Love from

A CAPFUL OF GLORY

By the same author

Gruesome Tide
The Monday Mutiny
Ninety Feet to the Sun
The Gemini Plot
Atlantic Encounter
The Eye of the Eagle
Secret of the Kara Sea

A CAPFUL OF GLORY

A Ben Grant Novel

ERIC J. COLLENETTE

WILLIAM KIMBER

© Eric J. Collenette 1988

All rights reserved. No part of it may be reproduced, stored in a retrieval system or transmitted, in any form or by any means, electronic, mechanical, photocopying, recording or otherwise, without prior permission in writing from William Kimber & Co Ltd.

First published in 1988

British Library Cataloguing in Publication Data

Collenette, Eric J.
A capful of glory
I. Title
823'.914 [F]

ISBN 0-7183-0701-1

*William Kimber & Co Ltd is part of the
Thorsons Publishing Group,
Wellingborough, Northamptonshire,
NN8 2RQ, England.*

Photoset in North Wales by
Derek Doyle & Associates Mold, Clwyd
and Printed in Great Britain by
Billing & Sons Limited, Worcester

1 3 5 7 9 10 8 6 4 2

Vaulting ambition, which o'er-leaps itself,
  And falls on the other.
    Macbeth, William Shakespeare, 1564–1616

I

Lieutenant-Commander Studding is an extremely efficient officer with the personality of a lamp-post. He looks like one too. Long-bodied, long-faced and long-nosed, with a stiff, round cap that sits on his head as though it belongs elsewhere. Nicknamed 'Starchy' by his crew, he is recognised as an ace amongst submarine captains, which is why he has been chosen to orchestrate 'Operation Showcase,' a theatrical performance to impress high-ranking politicians, visiting dignitaries, reporters, and hangers-on. Today's matinée is about to take place somewhere off St Catherine's Point.

Our audience is ensconced on the flightdeck of a Fleet carrier sailing on a parallel course three cables to starboard, and the whole routine begins with an emergency dive, after which we raise both periscopes and radar masts whilst submerged, followed by a short period of 'snorting' with clouds of spray and exhaust spewing out to delight the spectators. Finally we perform our *pièce de résistance*.

The depth gauges show fifty feet and it is up to Petty Officer Solomon, our second coxswain, and myself to hold her at this depth with the hydroplanes for as long as we can against the boat's natural tendency to surface. It is an old wartime trick adapted to create a spectacular climax, and the gun's crew is already closed up in their tower, holding rounds of blank ammunition; poised to burst out of the hatch the moment it opens. The captain will be out of the conning-tower even before they are, with his saluting party dressed in their best white sweaters.

'Surface!'

Jimmy's calm voice brings an immediate reaction. The big, black needles sweep round the dials, and nothing will hold her down now, so I leave my seat and nudge the cook sideways from the helmsman's seat, where he is doing the gun-layer's job while the boat is at 'gun-action stations'.

The whistle shrills, followed at once by the thump of the upper hatch, and a cold rush of air chills the control-room. The diesels choke, stutter, then rumble into their stride as a deluge of sea water splashes down from the tower. Guns and his crew will get soaked as they push out onto their platform, but the increased pressure inside the boat will keep most of it out.

The control room log keeper holds a bucket under the gaping mouth of my voicepipe as I drain it down. The boat takes her first roll, recovers, and rolls again as the sound of the first shot thumps in my ears, followed by two more at precise intervals. A perfect drill is brought to its climax with the shrill of three bos'n's calls as we salute the big aircraft carrier and turn away to port.

These welded boats are noted for their lively performance in a rough sea, due to the rounded bilges and the 'saddle' ballast tanks, but there are compensating comforts in the improved layout when compared to the old 'T' and 'S' boats we have all grown to respect. Few men need to sling hammocks in the fore-ends amongst the spare torpedoes anymore, and no one sleeps two to a bunk. We have closed-in heads and even a shower – although we have to obtain permission to use it when on extended patrols. Add two air-conditioning plants beneath the control-room deck, and living conditions are better than we have grown used to in other boats.

The experts tell us that *Audacity* and her sisters are far superior to their predecessors, and we have to believe them. The 'A' boats are six feet longer than the 'T's, and about forty tons heavier. They are three knots faster on the surface, with a thousand extra miles' range at eleven knots. We have ten torpedo tubes and a four-inch gun – exactly the same as the 'T,' but we can dive much deeper. However, in the true traditions of seamen, no one has a good word to say for them.

We are finished for the day now, so once we fall out from diving stations I get the men turned to, clearing up the boat for harbour, while Petty Officer Solomon musters his casing party up top, to clean brasswork after it has been submerged all day, and prepare the mooring hawsers ready for berthing. We have a training class from 'Dolphin Two' on board who move from one position to another, learning how to handle various controls under the supervision of our own lads. Each week of their training period they will go to sea in a boat, alternating between the three different types, so that when they pass their exams at the end of it all they will take up their duties in an operational boat with a basic knowledge of how it works.

They are experienced men who have served time in general service ships, so it is a conversion course really, and they soon become used to the relaxed, close-knit atmosphere, where a matey crowd is always ready to help, and they learn to work without supervision for most of the time.

It is this air of comradeship and professional pride that keeps men like me in submarines, and holds me back from going for promotion when it is offered, for I know that once I give up my 'chief' status and don the eight-buttoned jacket of an officer's uniform my submarine days are numbered. Lately however, the pressure for me to take the qualifying course is coming from a new source, and I am struggling with a tangle of indecision.

'Grant!'

Lieutenant Andy Tyson, our Jimmy the One, is calling from the wardroom, so I slide out into the passage, straighten my jacket and go next door to the small compartment where he sits in his fur-lined fighter-pilot's jacket that he always wears over grey flannel trousers while at sea. He has discarded his sporting flat cap with the earflaps, and his face is the colour and texture of a ripe strawberry. Tyson is a flamboyant character. The gunlayer swears that he wasn't born, but was scraped out of a concrete mixer. Nevertheless, his blunt, no-nonsense, gravelly voice commands respect from everyone, and he is known to be scrupulously fair-minded: a seaman right down to his rubber-soled sneakers. Many a time he and I have bent the rules to bale wayward inebriates from the clutches of over-zealous shore authorities, but let anyone try to pull a fast one, and he breathes fire.

Now he points to the leather bench opposite him, and I slip my knees under the baize-covered table. He waits until I am settled before leaning forward as though he has something confidential to tell me.

'I have a signal that concerns you, Grant.' There is a curious expression in his tone and face. Personal communications for ratings are unusual; and one from Captain S/M himself is like a summons from The Almighty. 'You have to report to Captain Kevel's office, fully booted and spurred, at oh nine four five tomorrow.'

'Aye aye, sir,' I respond tightlipped, ignoring the inquisitive look in his eyes. For a mere NCO like me to be called for by the great man is cause for concern. Could it be that I have chosen to go above the heads of my immediate superiors with a personal gripe? I know full well what is going through his head but it is none of his bloody business, and although I have a notion of why I have been sent for, I do not feel inclined to tell him more than I have to.

'That's all you have to say?'

'Yes, sir.'

He sniffs. 'Well you didn't jump out of your socks, so I assume that you know what it is all about. Have we got to wait to read about it in the national press?'

'I'm not sure what it is, sir. However, if it's what I suspect, then I'm afraid it is a personal matter.'

He grunts irritably. 'Well it is a bloody nuisance as far as I'm concerned, because it means that I have to take the spare-crew coxswain and leave you inboard for a day. What the hell have you done, for God's sake: kicked the admiral's cat, or raped his daughter?'

His attempt to humour the situation is supposed to loosen my tongue, but I am a reticent bastard when I decide to be. He drags the silence out for as long as he can, but in the end has to give in. 'You are a tight-lipped so-and-so, Grant. If I didn't know you better I would think you were jumping over my head with a complaint of your own.'

'It's nothing like that, sir,' I say with a grin. 'In fact I know little more than you at the moment, but it wouldn't do any good to try and guess.'

He sighs. 'All right. Clear off. I have to get cleaned into my harbour togs.'

I start to slide out, but he holds up his hand to stop me. 'One other thing while I have you here. If I catch the trot sentry pissing over the side again I will personally castrate him. Tell the lazy sods to use the pig's ear. That's all.'

Back in the chiefs' mess I settle down with some paperwork; trying to focus my mind on a list of requisitions to shut out the forebodings that try to invade my skull.

*

Captain Kevel has shale-oil running through his veins, and a chestful of medals earned doing wartime escapades that make my hair stand on end. He took boats into places where sane men would think twice about taking a rowing boat, and added symbols to his 'Jolly Roger' at twice the rate of other skippers. Despite his rashness he never lost a boat, and his men worshipped him. He is a man of dour countenance and penetrating eyes that seem to bore into a man's soul. He runs the flotilla with a mixture of iron discipline and humane understanding that only men of special quality can achieve. Everyone knows that his black Mercedes runs on submarine diesel oil, but no one would dream of questioning him or his old ex-coxswain driver,

Woody Birch, about it. The two men have a relationship dating back to their wild days in the Mediterranean, when they and other tenacious submariners were causing Rommel headaches as they severed his supply lines.

To stand in the presence of such a man is enough to send a thrill running through me. He is one of that special band of men who stay cool, and make calculated decisions with the knowledge that forty odd blokes are depending on his judgement as they are taken blindly into a situation where imagination plays as big a part as eyes and ears, when surface predators range in with probing, electronic fingers seeking out their slow-moving target in order to blast it out of existence. Tomorrow I will meet him, and it causes some misgivings. I decide to take some time out to be alone with my thoughts, and I know just the place.

Once we are secured alongside the trots at 'Blockhouse,' I make sure the sentries are organised for the night, while the engineroom brigade and electricians put on a standing charge for the morning. That done I go ashore to a small pub I know in Gosport where the lounge is warmed by an open fire, and a friendly host will not intrude on my thoughts unless invited. There I can knock back half a dozen whiskies in peace and work out what's running through my brain. Tomorrow I need to have my mind clear and my answers ready, for my whole future could depend on it. The connotations swim through my head like a bagful of worms. I have come to a cross-road and I do not know which way to turn. I have a feeling that my meeting with Captain S/M is going to bring that decision to a head.

At eight o'clock I watch *Audacity* slide out of her berth with the dew still dark and wet on her casing. Tyler waves a hand at me as she sounds three toots on her whistle to tell everyone she is going astern on her motors. The casing party look clean and smart as they line up, tallest forward, shortest aft, although the stocky shape of Solomon spoils it all when he takes up his position at the head of the group.

He is a slow-witted man. On the odd occasion when he has

wasted a few unnecessary words he has tended to make himself unpopular with certain pompous seniors with his blunt manner. Mainly because he cannot think of what to say, and the result usually turns out to be a cock-up. For all his rigid conformation he is well liked amongst his mates, and he has been on top line for promotion for a long time. It would mean becoming coxswain of his own boat, and there are doubts about his brain-power which has held him back so far. Now, however, Studding feels that his reliabilty and clean record is enough to overcome his shortcomings and has recommended him for advancement. My suspicious mind leads me to believe that the captain's motives are a little more devious than that.

Sometimes I have the feeling that *Audacity* is too good to be true. It is almost impossible to find fault with any of her company, and if, like Solomon, someone turns out to be under par he gets a quick transfer. It is as though this boat has been selected as an example of excellence; a model of proficiency, with no room for anything less than top grade. On the face of it that sounds good: A boat full of specially picked men with unblemished records and glowing references must be good. Until you suddenly miss the extrovert characters that usually make up a crew.

Every boat has its quota of 'skates' who can be a pain in the arse at times. They put an extra quality into a company that cannot be defined, yet is essential. They inject a certain humanity that keeps us down to earth. They are missing from this crew, and we are the poorer for it in my opinion.

The standards required from a submariner are high. People who are considered doubtful are placed on probation when they leave training until they prove themselves, and very few no-hopers slip through the net. Therefore, there is no reason for one particular boat to reap the best of the harvest at the expense of other crews.

She is clear of Haslar Creek now, and swinging her high bow to line up with the harbour mouth. A burst of blue exhaust explodes from her tail as the diesels stutter into life and take over from the electric motors. She has the profile of a Yanky boat, except for her raised prow, and she looks extremely handsome in the sunlight, but she has yet to earn the affection of those who man her, and it will take more than air-conditioning and closed-in toilets to cure their prejudice.

I turn away as she runs out through the gate, followed by a bustling Isle of Wight ferry. Already the next submarine is backing out of her berth as normal daily routine gets under way. The trots are beginning to dry out as the sun gets higher and there is still a steady stream of men toting gear down to their boats. I have two hours to waste before my interview and my feet automatically take me to the chiefs' mess in the barracks where the messmen are cleaning up the remains of breakfast.

They glare at me; trying to browbeat me out so that they can have a general clean-up, so I make my way up onto the ramparts where I can look out towards Spithead and run my eyes along the line of Southsea front and the buoyed channel until I locate the two boats. They are approaching their first turn to starboard before they run out towards Nab Tower and the open sea. *Audacity* is in the lead, though it is hard to tell from here. The sea is mottled with white-caps, and sparkling in the bright sunlight that turn the boats into dark shadows that seem to be suspended in a welter of jewels.

Solomon and Subby will have almost completed their check to make sure the hawsers are well secured under the casing. They have received a dousing from the exhausts when they reached her stern for the wind is driving in from the beam, but they will not skimp their work, because they know that one loose hawser could bring disaster to a dived boat.

I get a feeling of guilt as I watch them go. Fifteen years service has not robbed me of that feeling when I see my own boat go to sea without me. It took me three years to convince the navy to allow me back into submarines again. Numerous interviews with unsympathetic first lieutenants and captains who could see no sane reason why someone should wish to return to this life after such a long time, and were convinced that it would mean a retrogade step in my career. It was waste of my talent they told me. Experienced NCOs were needed to train new men into the ways of the navy. One captain even suggested that it was morally wrong, for in his eyes I would deprive a would-be submarine PO of the chance to pick up a coxswain's job.

I persisted anyway, with no qualms at all, and eventually I had my way, but now there is another threat to my peace of mind, and I find myself arguing the same old battle with people determined to kick me aft to the quarterdeck. They seem unable to understand that for me to become an officer would be like starting all over again in an alien world where I just don't belong, probably ending up in barracks or on a big ship, where I would be stifled amongst all the bullshit and mindless anonymity. I gave up trying to reason with those who cannot, or will not, see my point of view, and earned a reputation for being a stubborn bastard: a no-hoper with an unblemished service record, a tarnished DSM, and sod-all ambition. A combination that no one seems able to swallow.

I could have stuck to my guns if I had not met Zoe in the Pay-Master's office at HMS Drake. If that paybob had not been half an hour late for our appointment and I had not got into conversation with her I would have no problem. Even then our relationship should have ended when I went off on a two and a half year commission in the Med, but she was still waiting when I sailed back home again. She even understood and respected my reasons for refusing promotion. It was her family who put the pressure on, without even realising it.

It is not her fault that her old man is a millionaire inventor, with a knighthood and a huge estate in Hertfordshire. She kept it to herself for as long as our relationship was not too serious, then laughed at my misgivings when she told me. Her father is a self-made man with no pretensions at all, more at home in the company of brick-layers than the aristocracy; and her mother is an angel. In their naive way they can see no problems and are quite prepared to accept me into the family, with no reservations whatever.

It is the elder of her two brothers who throws a dampener over everything. Lieutenant-Commander Calvin Hope is a Sea Otter pilot, expert polo player and man about town, extremely conscious of his status in society, and knows how incongruous a chief petty officer's uniform can look in an assembly where most of the service guests are of flag rank. The odd thing is that most of Sir John's gold-braided mates seem quite happy to accept me as part of the family, but Calvin and his circle of toffee-nosed colleagues make no secret of the fact that they see my motives for latching on to Zoe as not entirely romantic.

I will say this for Calvin; he is perfectly honest about it when he makes his views known to Zoe and me. It is the only time I see her lose her natural exuberance, for she loves her brothers dearly, and when he says we are building a lot of grief for ourselves and the family, it hits home. Even though she hotly denies it I can see how much his words hurt. The only thing for me to do is to take the qualifying exams and try to become an officer. Zoe argues every step of the way when I say this to her. In her eyes I am betraying my own ideals for the wrong reasons, for I have always stressed vigorously my feelings about leaving submarines and losing my mates. She is convinced that we can make it work despite her brother's jaundiced comments. She is all for telling the rest of the mob to go to hell, but I am not so sure that she really knows the implications. I certainly do not want to be the cause of splitting up the family.

These are the thoughts running through my mind as I stride along the plush-carpeted, hushed corridor where framed photographs of by-gone submarines hang at intervals to remind me of where I am. I knock softly on the oak-panelled door and enter the outer office of Captain S/M. A prim leading Wren secretary glances up, and her brief, standard-pattern smile fades when she sees a lowly CPO grinning back at her. She is not used to entertaining underlings, and just manages to quell a disparaging smirk before it breaks surface.

'I know who you are,' she interposes when I lean forward to introduce myself. 'Take a seat. I will tell Captain Kevel that you are here.'

She wrinkles her pert little nose, gathers up some papers, and crosses over to tap on the inner door before easing her shapely frame inside. I am left to study the paintwork and twiddle my thumbs for a few minutes, then she is back again, refusing to look at me as she orders me to go in with a plummy, manufactured accent. How she gets on with Woody Birch, who is a law unto himself, with little polish, and even less refinement, is beyond me. It is said that Woody and the captain are like old shipmates when they are on their own, and the old chief is treated like part of the family.

I know that even one gold band on my sleeve would have allowed her to hold the door open for me, but today she is not going to become contaminated with a member of the lower order. It matters not, Snobby little bitches like her go through life with a bad smell under their noses, and they make me appreciate the Zoes of this world.

Inside the office there is a rich aroma of cigar-smoke and fine leather. Two high windows have blinds pulled halfway down to keep the atmosphere cool and easy on the eyes. A heavy, well-polished, ornately carved desk dominates, with an array of photographs and artefacts spread across the top. Behind it sits the great man himself, shirtsleeved and staring up at me from beneath bushy eyebrows, his expression stern and blunt. Behind him in the shadows between the drapes, Woody is watching me too, and our eyes meet for a second or two; just long enough for him to lower one eyelid in a surreptitious wink.

'Sit down, Grant,' invites Captain Kevel.

I squat in the chair facing him while he leans forward to place his elbows on the desk, surveying me with his penetrating grey eyes. I hold his gaze, refusing to be brow-beaten, until a slow smile flickers across his lips.

'I am going to be quite informal,' he says quietly. 'I am an old friend of Sir John and Lady Hope, and I bounced Zoe on my knee when she was a pup. I love them all very much, and I do not wish to see them hurt. Therefore, I feel entitled to stick in my oar. I am not going to lecture you on the difficulties you will encounter when you marry the girl: God knows, I am out of my depth here anyway! However I do know that you are being bombarded from all sides, and you have no family of your own to consult. That is why I have invited Birch along, because I believe you and he are cast in the same mould. Perhaps between us we can work something out and reach an understanding. Let me say at once that you are quite at liberty to tell me to mind my own business, and then go your own way. I assure you, nothing more will be said.

'However, before you do I want you to know that this meeting is entirely off the record, and that my only concern is for the future happiness and well-being of my god-daughter.' He fidgets uneasily in his chair. 'I don't mind telling you that I have never played this kind of role before, and I am finding it bloody hard going. So, if you wish to terminate this interview I shall be very much relieved.'

I glance over at Woody, but his expression tells me nothing. So I stare down at the desk for a moment, running the captain's words through my head before looking up to meet his eyes again. 'I do need to talk to someone, sir. The implications of what Zoe and I are doing wriggle about inside my brain like a bag of worms. I feel as though I am out on a limb, alienated from my shipmates, and encroaching on a world in which I have no part.'

I look straight into his eyes. 'Don't get me wrong, sir. I don't suffer from an inferiority complex. In fact, to be honest, I will lose some prestige if I go for promotion as far as I am concerned. Like you though, I can see that Zoe doesn't know what she is getting into, and the last thing I want is to make her unhappy.'

He nods slowly. 'That is the kind of straight talking I like. I won't offer advice; you have had more than enough of that already. What do you intend to do about it?'

'*Audacity* is due to join the Far East Fleet soon, sir. A two and a half year commission would allow time to sort things out.'

His face hardens and he glowers at me. 'I see,' he says with heavy sarcasm as he glances over his shoulder at Woody. 'We are back on that tack again, are we?' He slams a hand down on the desk with enough force to rattle the windows. 'Damn it, Grant. My time is too valuable to waste on you!'

' 'Ang on, sir!' Woody breaks in quickly as he steps forward from the shadows. 'It ain't so easy for Ben. You ain't told 'im what's on your mind.'

It takes a moment or two for Kevel to calm down. This is an unnerving experience for both of us, and without Woody it would have come to a sticky end right then. The captain huffs and puffs for a moment, then jerks his head up sharply. 'Let us get one thing straight, Grant. Whatever the circumstances I will never pull strings for anyone: That's not my way. What I am telling you now has nothing whatever to do with what we have discussed so far.'

He takes a drink from a glass of water as he regains composure. 'A new era is dawning in submarines, and we are being dragged kicking and screaming into the modern world despite the tight purse-strings of the Government. Two new, experimental boats are in the pipeline, using the Hydrogen-peroxide power that the Germans tried out. They will be 'X' class boats, and the boffins tell us they will do thirty knots dived.' He sees my expression alter and holds a hand up quickly.

'I know – I know. The stuff is lethal if not handled correctly. That is why we need all the experienced men we can get. There are other changes coming in that I cannot even talk about, always supposing I understood half of it anyway. We are to have a new one-hundred foot practice escape tank to replace the old fifteen foot absurdity, along with many other innovations. In short, Grant, we are launching into a new era, and will require men like you to make it all come together.'

He is warming to his subject as he looks into the future. Like me he is steeped in submarines. 'Your name was on the short-list long before this business with Zoe came about. We believe that your experience is under-utilised at present, and eventually you would have received counsel from your captain, with recommendation to take examinations for a commission. Should you qualify you would become part of a team of specialists running an extensive training programme. All I am doing now is to short-circuit the system in the hope that it may help you to decide on your future.'

He slumps back into his chair. 'I have a vested interest, for I am to become very much involved in the training, and I need men I can trust to combat the interference of government "experts". We all know what they can do to a project like this.' He is well into his pet subject now.

'Our destiny is being shaped by politicians, Grant. Farmers, shop-keepers, and city men who do not know one end of a torpedo from the other. Tea-drinking, desk-bound merchants with verbal diarrhoea and inflated egos. The trick is to gain their support with show-pieces, like *Audacity* laid on yesterday, and which you and I know is as close to reality as Santa Claus. Then, when they have searched their purses and committed themselves, make certain that they keep their sticky fingers out of it.'

He is breathing heavily now, and Woody is grinning widely in the background. I smile back at him. A load is being lifted from my shoulders as a new world opens up. A future and a challenge is what is on offer. All I could hope for, and most important of all; the chance to remain in submarines and be of service. At last I have a legitimate excuse to throw aside my prejudices and go for a commission.

The captain is used to blowing his top on this subject and is slightly embarrassed when he gets carried away like this. 'Well – er – that's the full story,' he blusters. 'I can see that I have caught your interest so there is nothing more to add. If you wait for the official report to come through, *Audacity* will have sailed for China, and it will be too late. If you decide to accept this challenge you should put your request in within the next few days; and don't think it will be an easy ride. I want only the best, and no personal considerations will sway me from that. It is entirely up to you now.'

The interview is ended and he has resumed his mantle of authority, so I stand up to attention and he nods dismissal. Woody falls in beside me as I go out to where the snooty secretary busies herself at her typewriter. The old coxswain catches my look and lifts his eyebrows. There is a devilish twinkle in his eyes as he leans over her. 'You had better get used to this bloke, Penny. 'E's about ter become one of the aristocracy.'

He throws a crafty grin at me. 'Penny's old man drives a tram, Ben. She's never forgiven him for it.'

Outside the air smells dry and clean as the sun warms the parade-ground. We walk together in silence for a moment before Woody asks in a quiet voice. 'Reckon yer might become a "pig" then?'

'There's nothing to stop me now,' I reply without hesitation. 'It's everything I want. You can be my best man if you like.' I grin at him, but I am surprised to see him staring back with a deadly serious expression.

'Listen, Ben. I don't want ter be a wet blanket, but I've bin movin' abaht with that lot fer a long time and they treat me well, but they ain't all like the skipper. I know my place, and they find my accent amusing. I am a mixture of servant and mascot, and even the snobby bastards can accept that. You ain't gonna find it so easy. I have seen what happens to some blokes who try to push into the circle by pretending to be what they ain't. The trouble with you and the old man is that you've bin in boats too long. You've both forgotten what a shower of bastards some of these people can be. In the real world, mate, the gulf between us and them is vast. It is getting better, but you and Zoe have got some storms ahead of you – make no mistake.'

I walk soberly beside him for a few yards, then I slap him on the shoulder. 'Don't worry your head about me, Woody. One little half ring is not gonna change things too much.'

II

Nothing Woody or anyone can say will destroy this new feeling of relief and optimism that I have after my interview with Captain Kevel. It is Thursday morning on the twenty-ninth day of June 1950, and I decide to leave it until after the weekend before I put in my official request. That will allow time to telephone Zoe and arrange to meet so that I can tell her all about it. With my decision made I can get excited about the future, and I can hardly wait to share it with her. Everything is falling into place, and I know she will be just as thrilled as I am when she knows.

Routine checks are being carried out in *Aucacity* prior to sailing, and as I clatter down through the fore-hatch the diesels cut out as the engine-room brigade knock off the topping-up charge. There is the usual bustle of organised chaos that always exists when we are about to cast off, and when I go through the boat to check that the crew is all aboard I find the training class pairing up with our own men at their stations. That done I report to Tyson and take my place in the helmsman's seat.

There are a few raised eyebrows from the lads when they notice that I have lost my customary brusqueness. I am not noted for my jocularity when important routine is being carried out, and I usually clamp down on any unnecessary chit-chat. Today, however, nothing can upset me, for I feel that for once the navy is treating me right, and that if that is cause for a few suggestive nudges and undercover winks. I don't give a damn.

I hardly notice the navigator drop through the conning tower hatch in flurry of arms and legs.

'Coxswain!' he pants when he has sorted himself out. 'Belay all preparations for sea. Today's exercises are cancelled and the training class must return to Dolphin Two. We will revert to harbour routine, and the ship's company will fall in on the jetty at oh nine double oh. I think the captain is to address us.' He shrugs at my puzzled expression. 'Don't ask me; I'm just as bewildered as you are. Maybe the Russians have finally blown their tops.' He gives a weak grin; but I can see nothing to smile at.

There is an ominous nausea growing inside my belly, along with a surge of cold anger, for I have the feeling that the bastards have done it to me again. I have not heard a news broadcast this morning, but I do know that there is concern about goings-on in some remote country on the other side of the world called Korea. It sounds like a local skirmish, and I cannot imagine how it can affect me. Perhaps his little joke is nearer the truth than he realises. Maybe some bloody idiot has started a real war. When I go up top I notice that the other boats have also secured from 'sea stations,' and their training classes are mustered on the jetty, ready to follow our lot back to their own barracks.

'What the hell's going on?' Hancock, the torpedo gunner's mate, is standing beside me. 'Look, they are clearing lower deck in Dolphin.'

I follow his gaze, and surely enough, even from here we can get a glimpse between the buildings of men rushing out to fall in on the big parade-ground. There is an air of expectancy amongst our lot as they emerge from below to stand gaping about as their routine is spoiled.

Five minutes before time the crew is already drawn up in three ranks on the jetty beside the boat, and I hardly need to call the roll to know that every man is present. Promptly at nine o'clock Studding arrives to receive his report from Tyson, and all other sound seems to die as he takes up position in front of us with his face set in a serious expression.

He takes out a note-pad. 'I have jotted down the details as

they came to me,' he announces firmly. 'They are as follows.'

We wait while he checks his notes. I can hear other voices reading out what sounds like a proclamation to other crews. They sound sharp and crisp in the morning air, while an uncanny stillness hangs over the barracks to allow the harbour noises to invade this little back-water.

'On the twenty-fifth of June North Korean troops crossed the Thirty-Eighth Parallel in an unprovoked attack against their South Korean neighbours. It was a blatant act of naked aggression that took the army of South Korea completely off guard. Another Pearl Harbour, if you like. They have already captured the capital city of Seoul, and are pressing forward in an attempt to occupy the whole peninsula.'

He takes a breath before going on. 'On the twenty-seventh the Security council met and called on all members of the United Nations to send support to South Korea. Fifteen countries are involved, and as you would expect, Britain is to take her part; although the main contingent will come from the United States. Men who were due for release into the reserve will find that they are being kept on, and others, already back in civilian jobs are being recalled – it is as serious as that.'

He waits a moment, looking at our faces as though trying to read what goes on behind the blank stares. 'You may have to look at a map to find out where Korea is, but I can tell you that although it may seem remote, its importance cannot be over-estimated. This is the first real communist threat to the free world, and the first time the UN have been called upon to do what they were set up to do.' His voice takes on a note of pride. 'As I said before, the United States will take the brunt of it, but they are desperately short of battle-hardened veterans. So many Americans who were discharged only five years ago after fighting the Japs will find themselves dragged back to the Far East again to bolster their less experienced comrades. Britain's contribution is small in comparison, but I have no doubt we shall give a good account of ourselves.'

He takes another breath, and searches the faces of his men. Most of them wear medals on their chests when they fall in for Sunday Divisions. There has been little pause since the end of the last conflict and the signs of war are everywhere to be seen in Portsmouth. He knows that no fine words will drum up patriotic verve amongst this crowd. If there is a job to be done, then they will get on with it because they are professionals, not because someone tells them that they are being sent out to save the world.

When he continues his voice is even and matter-of-fact, for he has gauged the mood of his crew. '*Audacity*'s departure for the Far East has been brought forward, and I am afraid there is not enough time to allow for normal embarkation leave. It is up to the first lieutenant and the coxswain to work something out so that everyone gets as much time with his family as possible before we sail. If it is any consolation, I have a feeling that the whole thing will be over before we reach the war zone, although I tell you here and now that I have every intention of pushing the boat to the limit in an effort to play our part. The one good thing to come out of all this is that the United Nations seems to be working better than the League of Nations that failed so miserably before the war; so perhaps there is hope for us yet. I cannot disguise the fact that I am looking forward to an opportunity to prove ourselves in a real situation after all the hard work we have put into working up to full efficiency. That's all.'

Taken off-guard by his abrupt ending Tyson leaps to attention as the captain turns to go; barking us all rigid with an order that rebounds from the blank walls of the buildings before he salutes.

Studding stalks away as more sounds come from the barracks. Division by division the men are marched away to resume normal work, and there is a general buzz of chatter.

A gruff order from me silences our men. There are always a thousand things to do when we are lucky enough to get a spell alongside the wall, and very soon the crew is dispersed throughout the boat, carrying out overdue servicing and repairs.

When the first lieutenant turns up he has details for leave. We have ten days before we sail. So each watch will be allowed five days, with an overlap to allow travelling time for those who live in far away places. It means that most will spend at least three days with their families, and those who have no home ties are asked to forego their leave to ensure that the boat is in all respects ready for sea by the stipulated time.

Married men are given priority, and the bachelors amongst us swop duties to give them first chance to travel 'up the line.' Most officers have brought their wives down to local lodgings so they have no real problems. Some say that one day there will be married quarters for everyone, but to a cynical bastard like me that spells the beginning of the end. The very idea of most of the crew on 'R.A.'* with wives and kids waiting at the dockyard gate each time we sail in to port doesn't bear contemplation.

Sometime during the forenoon I find time to telephone Zoe at her office in Devonport, but before I can get a word in about Korea she interrupts.

'Uncle Tom told me that you might change your mind,' she says with a note of anxiety in her voice. 'I hope he didn't pressure you into anything. Remember, I want you the way you are, so don't think you have to do it for my sake.'

'It's nothing like that,' I tell her. 'I had almost decided to have a go, and all he did was to make the whole thing possible. However, there is a snag.'

She listens without a sound as I explain about Korea. So quiet I stop halfway through to ask if she's still there.

'Yes,' come the subdued reply. 'I am here.'

'It is only a small conflict,' I insist. 'It will probably fizzle out in a few days, and then they will send me home to take my exams. Nothing's really altered.'

---

* Rationed ashore.

There is a long pause. 'I see,' she says eventually, with no life in her voice.

'We have until Saturday week,' I add cheerfully. 'I can get a couple of days off.'

Again that long hesitation. 'I'm going away Ben. Dad has been invited to a conference in Austria, and we are making a holiday of it. I am due to fly out with them at the weekend.'

Now it is my turn to go silent with a new anger building up inside me. I should not need to ask her to change her plans in the circumstances.

'It's no fault of mine that this bloody war started, Zoe. I can't do anything about. It is a snag, but at least we can begin to make plans now.'

'You don't have to explain, Ben. I realise that you have no choice, and I'm sure everything will come right for us eventually. It is just that I promised Dad that I would go with him on this trip. You know how impatient he gets when he has to make speeches and mix with what he calls 'a lot of pompous penguins.' I cannot let him down now, or he won't go at all.'

'I understand,' I mumble, choking back an angry retort. 'I'll see you when I get back.'

I feel like slamming the receiver down on her for not putting me first. Neither of us speak for some time, and when the pips go I place the money in almost without thinking.

'Ben!'

'Yeah?'

'Give me until Saturday morning and I'll see what I can do. You must understand: it is for mother's sake mostly. Dad has turned down so many wonderful trips to places she always wanted to visit, and now she has a chance of a whole week in Vienna. All he needs is one tiny excuse to back out of this one, and if I so much as hint that I might not go with him he will do just that. I – I feel I must not let her down.'

My throat is tight. 'You must do what you think is right. I have to go now. We have a lot to do before Saturday week.

We will have to make this goodbye, Zoe.'

This time I do set the receiver down and stride away to the boat, bundling aside outraged sailors as I go, with that inner rage building inside like a furnace. I have given my life to the navy and it always seems to come up and hit me between the eyes when things are beginning to go my way. Inside the boat I launch into a pile of paperwork to get the first batch of men away on their leave with passes and travel warrants. As if to rub salt into my wounds the skipper decides to give another little pep-talk before they go. Normally he is a reticent sod, but when he decides to give one of his speeches there's no stopping him, and today I get the impression that he thinks this war is a gift from the gods, designed especially to put his boat to the test.

I listen with the others to him rambling on about proving ourselves in battle conditions, and sounding positively disheartened when he admits that there might not be a need for submarines out there. I wonder if the whole thing has not been drummed up by a few fire-eaters like him, who are looking for any excuse to put years of training into practice.

'Just one additional point,' he adds in his supercilious voice. 'You will know the way I do things, so you won't be surprised when I tell you that *Audacity* will be ready for sea before the set date. The coxswain and chief ERA will organise things so that the maximum effort is obtained, and I warn you that if anyone overstays his leave by as much as one minute, he will find himself in serious trouble. Remember, the ship is under sailing orders. If anyone has a genuine, serious problem he must go to the first lieutenant at once, for there will be no time to arrange replacements or compassionate leave after this weekend. In any case I would be most reluctant to replace any members of the crew at this late stage.'

I lose his words as my thoughts take off in other directions. I could put my fist through the pressure-hull when I think of it. A piddling little war in a piss-arsed country that nobody gave a damn about until now; and these war-mongering sods are talking about it as though it is the biggest thing in their lives. The rage that boils inside turns me into an uncompromising, moody sod as I prowl through the boat like a predator, picking on all and sundry, and refusing to listen to any excuses for shortcomings. Even my fellow NCOs stay well clear, and it isn't long before I find myself hauled up to the wardroom for a lecture from Tyson.

'Everything okay, Coxswain?' he asks carefully.

'Yes, sir.'

'Well then, what's got into you? Those lads do not deserve what you're giving them. Their leave has been curtailed, and they must be anxious about what lies ahead. Our job is to instil confidence and maintain morals. I will not have my NCOs bringing their personal problems into the boat, so either you get it out of your system, or I will do something about it.'

'Don't know what you mean, sir,' I lie sullenly. He will get no help from me.

'Oh yes you bloody well do. I do not wish to pry into your affairs, Grant, but your attitude must change considerably. Do I make myself absolutely clear?'

I draw myself upright and stare him in the eyes. 'There is nothing wrong with me, sir. I am determined to get the boat ready on time – that's all.'

'Well, you won't help matters by going about like a bear with a sore head. It has taken a long time to build the excellent spirit we have in the boat, and I will not allow you to ruin it. If you can't see what effect you are having on the troops, you are no better than one of those sea-going grocers who masquerade as coxswains. Think about it.'

'Aye aye, sir.' It's all I can say. Deep down I know he is right, but I am in no mood to admit it.

'Before you go I must tell you that there have been two requests to remain behind on compassionate grounds, and I believe them to be genuine. The chief ERA has a sick wife whose condition is causing concern, and the signalman has marital problems. The welfare people have been on to me about both, so I have arranged for replacements. The one good thing to come out of it is that we are to get a warrant engineer to replace the chief.'

'Very well, sir.' This time I am obviously dismissed, so I make my way back to the mess. It will take a good bloke to replace the chief, even if he is a warrant officer. He and I have always been good mates, yet when it comes down to it I know little about him. I did not even know he had a wife; let alone a sick one. He is a quiet man with impassive features that discourage personal talk, and keep him slightly apart from his mess-mates, but he takes an exceptional pride in his job. He will be sorely missed.

The moment the last man disappears with his leave pass and warrant the boat comes alive with the hustle and bustle of preparations for 'going foreign.' I immerse myself in work to shut out the niggling thoughts that threaten to take over, but by Saturday I can stand no more of it. I know that if I don't see Zoe before we sail I will never shake off my morbidity. So, with a sort of anxious panic urging me along I set off for Hertfordshire, hoping to catch her before the family leave for the Continent.

Calvin meets me halfway along the elm-lined drive that leads up to the old Tudor manor that squats amongst a maze of gardens and yew hedges in the crook of the arm of a meandering river. It is picture-postcard English countryside, with orchards and dairy farms spreading out on all sides.

'If you are looking for Zoe I'm afraid you are too late, old chap.' Both he and the thoroughbred he is riding look down at me over their long noses, and I am suddenly aware of the sweat that soaks into my shirt beneath my thick uniform jacket. He wears riding breeches and open-necked shirt, with a flat cap sitting squarely across his proud, handsome face, looking very much the country squire.

'Well, Ben,' he drawls, doing his best to keep the sneer out of his voice. 'Zoe tells me that you have finally decided to go for promotion and we are to become brothers-in-law.' There is a catch in his voice, as though the phrase 'brothers-in-law' sticks in his throat.

I am too disappointed about missing Zoe to find an answer, so I focus on a herd of Friesians grazing complacently in a nearby meadow. There is a hard knot in my gullet and I am in no mood for his patronising chatter.

'If you would like to walk with me to the house we could drink to your forthcoming promotion. You don't mind if I don't dismount, do you?'

'That would be a bit premature –' I choke, on the verge of calling him 'sir.' Old habits are hard to break, and I cannot forget that he is a two-and-a-half-ringer. 'We have been ordered to the Far East ahead of time because of this Korean business, and I was hoping to see Zoe before we sailed.'

The horse stumps impatiently in a half-circle so that I am faced with its backside while he makes small effort to regain control. 'Well I'm blowed!' he exclaims as he struggles with rein and stirrup. 'I too have had sailing orders. I am to go with *Neptune*. Didn't realise they were sending submarines though. Wouldn't have thought there was much call for them.' A shrewd expression crosses his face. 'How will it affect your prospects of early promotion then?'

The horse has turned so that I can feel the hot breath blasting from its nostrils – and it stinks. I reach up to grab the bridle, determined to keep it from sticking its arse into my face again, and to show it who's boss. Calvin's eyes narrow as they dart quickly to my hand, and for a second I think he is about to react, but he bites back his indignation.

I look up at him. 'It will have to be postponed for a while I reckon.'

'Damned shame!' He sticks his tongue into his cheek, bulging it out while he stares down at me from a great height over the flicking ears of the horse. A noisy crowd of crows set up a raucous chatter in the elms, and the sweat runs down my face. When I lift my free hand to mop it the horse shies away. I hold on tight, and the sod has a go at my hand.

'Steady!' he barks, and I get the impression that he is warning me, and not the nag.

When all is back in order again he returns to the subject with a smirk. 'That's unfortunate. However, it will allow time for you to think things over. Wouldn't do to rush into it. You may find it quite a transition to enter officer country after all your time with the troops. Quite a jump from the chiefs' mess. I have met some very unhappy warrant officers who found that they were out of their depth in a new world. It must be quite disconcerting to find yourself at the bottom of the pile after being King of the Roost.'

His face hardens, and there is a cold, malevolent twist to his mouth. Both he and his horse hate my guts. 'My concern is for Zoe, Ben. In the past you've made no secret about your reluctance to take promotion. So I hope you are doing it now for the right reasons.'

There is an underlying threat in his tone and I have difficulty forgetting that in my world he wears two and a half gold rings on his sleeve, and will soon wear gold braid on his cap – just one step down from God. Somehow, in the cold light of day I cannot think of him as my brother-in-law.

'Well, like you say, I have got time to think about it,' I murmur, almost beneath my breath.

I turn away, sick of the whole thing. Right now I want no part of any of them, not even Zoe. Perhaps he is right. Maybe they are too rich for my blood. I feel my background, and the long years of serving on the lower deck weighing on my shoulders. I feel his arrogant stare on my back as I turn to walk back down the long drive. There is nothing more to be said, and we both know it. He makes no attempt to delay me as I trudge towards the main road.

Back at the boat I try, without success, to concentrate on a new stack of paperwork. Eventually I throw it aside and go up top for a breather. It is a half hour into the second dog watch, and the quiet gloom of evening spreads a calmness across the trots. The only people in sight are the trot-sentries pacing the cold steel casing. I nod response to ours and clunk forward to the very eye of the boat. Right up on the prow with six torpedo tubes and a free-flooding buoyancy tank beneath my feet. That tank catches us out at times when we dive, for it holds the air until we can force her bows down with 'planes. Until, with a suddenness that seems especially designed to catch us out, it floods up, and if we are not on the ball, takes us down into a steep dive that is hard to control. The high bow was added when the first boats performed badly in rough weather, and is meant to aid stability. In *Audacity* we have reason to curse it every so often.

I turn to place my feet either side of the towing trough, looking aft along her length. Two short lengths of white-painted cable lead out through the bullring, shackled to emergency towing wires that are clamped along the casing and on up to the lip of the bridge with soft metal clips. They would enable a tow to be picked up when the weather is too rough for men to work on the casing.

The four-inch gun stares back at me from beneath the periscope standards and the front of the bridge, with its tompion providing a splash of colour above the ship's bell.

I stride aft past the capstan and the retracting bollards. Unlike the rounded blister tanks on the 'T' and 'S' boats the broad expanse of the ballast tanks spread out on each side to allow an easy walking platform, and they help to make these 'A's roll like buckets in any kind of a swell. I grab the brass rail that runs along the side of the bridge – always the first thing to be polished when we surface at the end of a day's exercise – easing my body aft until I reach the snort-mast.

I have never met a submariner who had a good word to say for the 'snort.' Apart from a natural aversion to extra holes in the pressure-hull we are always conscious of the fact that when it is raised it has to withstand the drag of the ocean as it vibrates to the throb of the diesels as they suck air down through the induction tube and expels burnt gases through the exhaust. In theory it is perfectly safe, with built-in protection that prevents water from entering the boat, but we have already had problems with sea-water getting into the engine-cylinders when we have to dive in a hurry.

The type we have has a device roughly similar to a lavatory cistern that shuts off the induction valve whenever the mast dips beneath the surface. It stops the ocean coming in all right, but unfortunately it also cuts the flow of air, so that the diesels suck a vacuum in the boat that threatens to drag out our eardrums. In a rough sea, when the mast keeps getting swallowed up in the swell, this can prove to be a prolonged, painful process.

The advantage they tell us, is that we are able to remain dived while charging batteries to reduce our silhouette. In these days of improved radar this advantage is limited, and many, like me, remain unconvinced.

Once clear of the bridge I stroll out on to the after end of the casing and find another thoughtful soul standing on his own, staring out across the harbour. Hancock is a crabby-faced individual with a personality to match. Like me he has spent most of his time in submarines and thinks of general service as an alien world. He swings round when he hears me coming, and the look of annoyance fades when he sees who it is.

'What ho, Ben!' he greets, and turns back to study the traffic criss-crossing the pool.

'What are you up to?' I ask with a smirk. 'I thought you would be down below with the "experts." '

'Stuff the "experts!" Those poxy "barrack-stanchions" know where to find me if I'm wanted.' He spits over the side. 'It's fuckin' "experts" that got us into this mess.'

I have to grin. 'How do you work that out?'

He swings on me again, and his face is serious enough to drain my smile. 'I was talkin' to an "expert" about this bloody war we're goin' to, and it makes no sense to me. I am a simple bloke, Ben. There's no bastard in this bucket who knows more than me about my bloody torpedoes, but when it comes to working out what makes politicians tick I'm as thick as a dredger's bilge. This "expert" was sayin' that Korea is roughly the same size as Britain, and right up to 1945 it was independent. Well; when the war came to an end some clever sod decided to draw a line along the Thirty-Eighth Parallel and say, "You lot to the north will be communists from now on, and all you lot to the south will be capitalists." '

He chuckles bitterly. 'Can you imagine it? It was like drawin' a line between "scouse-land" and The Wash to try and split England in two.'

He stops for a moment as his mind tries to come to grips with it, then goes on almost as though he is talking to himself. 'The daft thing is that it worked. Within five years they've got the Koreans at each other's throats. It is as if that lot from Yorkshire and Lancashire northwards are scrappin' us southerners.' He stares into my eyes with his forehead creased into an intense frown. 'How do they do it, Ben? How do these politicians draw a line between two communities and set them against each other?'

I think for a moment. I know that what he says is over-simplified, and that if I was a clever bloke I could find deeper reasons for what has happened. The snag is that after the clever bastards have worked it all out it is simple sods like us who have to go out and clear up the mess. I take the easy way out and slap a hand on his shoulder. 'You think too much, Torps.'

'In other words, you're just as stupid as I am.'

'That's right.'

I leave him standing there with his problems. Somehow the chat has cheered me up a bit. The fresh air is getting to my lungs and clearing away the sourness. Perhaps it isn't so bad after all. A few days at sea will put things into perspective, and I've always been a sucker for new places. In a few days time we will be churning our way southward, and I can look forward to seeing a part of the world that I know only from books. Other men seem able to take it all as a matter of course, but the idea of going ashore in places like China and Japan excites me.

I sidle past the bridge again and find the trot sentry staring ashore at an approaching figure who saunters casually down towards the jetty. As I watch I notice something familiar about his gait that pulls me up short of the fore-hatch. As he draws nearer my newfound sense of well-being vanishes. I swing away from the hatch and take a couple of steps toward the gang-plank, trying hard not to believe my eyes.

'Welks!' I blurt out as the squat shape crosses to the casing and stands in front of me with an evil grin on his face.

'Mister Welks to you, Chief Petty Officer Grant. Or "sir" if you like. And while we are about it, I am entitled to a salute.'

The same whining, nasal voice, and the same sly-eyed, glowering stare as he gloats over me. A deep, empty feeling of despair overcomes me as I look at this spectre from the past. This evil bastard should have been kicked out of submarines long ago if there was any justice. Now, here he stands in his officer's uniform with his sneering face a yard from mine, and I know he must be the new warrant officer the first lieutenant spoke about.

For one brief moment I wonder if I can find a good excuse to ask for a transfer. The thought of serving in the same boat as this contemptible reptile crushes me. Almost subconsciously I give a sloppy salute and try to ignore the gleam of triumph that flashes across his smarmy features. I step back to allow him to precede me down through the fore-hatch. My world seems to have collapsed again as I follow him like a zombie. How could any responsible service give this slimy sod a commission? This worthless rat who fought against me every step of the way when I was trying to bring home a crippled submarine with everything against me, should have been kicked out after the way he behaved. The irony is that it is probably my fault that he wasn't, for I was so grateful to come out of it alive I just could not bring myself to press charges. So he got away with it and now here he is: large as life and twice as ugly.

Back in the mess I shuffle through my papers, but they are utterly meaningless, for my mind is filled with this new calamity. After a while I give up and slope off ashore to the barracks. The radio is turned on, and a news-reader is talking about the South Koreans fighting against overwhelming odds and in full retreat.

'Good!' I think to myself. 'Maybe it will all be over before we get there, and I'll slap in a request to take the warrant officer's course so fast the ink won't have time to dry.'

There's two other chiefs in the mess, but they ignore me after I rebuff their overtures, and I settle into a corner of my own with a cup of strong tea, pretending to read a newspaper. The print is a blur and my head is filled with visions from the past. Men struggling in semi-darkness through filthy, oil-skimmed water. Trying to hold down a growing panic and retain their sanity as they squeeze through a tiny hatch into the cold Norwegian Sea. Haggard faces staring out of dark sockets into a merciless wind that freezes life out of their bodies while they crouch in a wilderness, trying to hug warmth into their miserable, emaciated frames.

Through it all comes the memory of that griping, nagging sod who plagued me every inch of the way; sucking the guts out of me as I wrestled with a situation that was beyond my capabilities; causing me to lose what little confidence I had, so that I prayed for something to come and lift the burden from me. I turn very cold, and a shiver runs through me when I recall how close I came to turning into a quivering jelly and giving into his snivelling persuasions to surrender and live out the war in some cosy POW camp.

The remainder of the evening passes in a haze, and it takes until daylight to get my mind into some sort of order again. I determine to get a grip on myself and try to ignore Welks. After all, there is no reason why our paths should cross too often if he keeps to his engine-room, while I stick to my own affairs up forward. It is a nice thought, but a futile one, for I know only too well that in the close confines of a submarine there is no dividing line between engine-room and upper-deck as there is in general service, and Welks is not the kind of man to forget the way I humiliated him, and made him look an incompetent idiot in front of his own subordinates and lost him his self-respect. He is here like a ghost from my past to haunt the guts out of me, and that small, thin gold ring he wear on his sleeve makes it all the more possible. Somehow, incredible as it would seem to a logical mind I know he is out to break me.

In the glaring light of a new day, however, I am in no mood to knuckle under to a toad like him. It was a kick in the gut to see him standing there after all these years, but now the intitial shock is gone, and I know that I am worth two of his sort. If anyone is going to break on this trip it will be Mister 'Bloody' Welks. I have a new notion running inside me today. Could it be that destiny has brought him here for his own come-uppance, and that in spite of his slimy smile he too has seen a ghost from the past, with more reason to be concerned, for I am a condemning witness to a period in his career that would be better left buried. Maybe I have been offered a second chance to see that he gets what he so richly deserves, and bring retribution for the memory of all those poor wretches who suffered because of his incompetence. The idea sends a strange warmth surging through me that I cannot fully understand, nor am I particularly proud of what I am feeling, for it smells of vengeance.

The time passes quickly as we draw our tropical kit and prepare the boat for sea. Soon there is a chronic shortage of space, even though we offload our spare torpedoes. It will be a long trip, and there is no attendant depot ship in which to stow our spare gear. So we utilise every inch of space to cram in the supplies we require for the six or seven week journey.

Too little time has elapsed since the end of the war to allow for any fuss to be made. Cinema newsreels show pictures of men carrying kit-bags up the gangway of HMS *Neptune,* but in general the whole thing is very low key. The carrier slips away from her berth alongside the dock-yard wall with her Marine band playing to a scattering of semi-official people waving or saluting from the jetty, and her men remain formed up on deck, trying to recognise a familiar face amongst the crowd who wave as she goes by Southsea front to her anchorage at Spithead, where she is to take on ammunition from lighters before making a quiet departure.

A group of senior officers comes to see us off. The other boats have already gone to sea with their training classes, and we are the star attraction. Even so, there is a minimum of formality and by the time we round the first buoy in the fairway most of the men are below and soup is being served. Except for a few 'natives' who remain up top for a last futile wave to wives and kids the boat settles into its normal sea routine.

III

Nab Tower comes abreast, and we wallow out into the open water of the Channel at a good fifteen knots, heading for our first port of call at Gibraltar. Above my head the solid crunch of a headsea sounds heavy on the casing and bridge and the occasional splash of water comes down the conning-tower. The skipper is in a hurry, making no allowance for the sea, so we thump our bow into the rollers, sending clouds of spray over the men on the open bridge. When I go up top during the first watch a blood-red sun is beckoning us on towards the south-west, and we are ploughing into the rollers with exploding cliffs of brilliant white spray hurtling aft to swamp the bridge while cataracts of foaming water spews out of the drain holes onto the ballast tanks.

It is an exhilarating experience. My feet are only about eleven feet above sea-level as she plunges along, and when she rolls the crests seem to come level with my shoulders. She is a solid, compact unit, designed to sail through the ocean rather than over it, knifing into the swells and shouldering them aside as she buries her slim body for long periods while the diesels suck great quantities of air and sea down through the tower with greedy gurgling sounds. If necessary we can shut the upper hatch and use the inductors, but that is unpopular, for it isolates the men on the bridge from their mates below, so we prefer to mop up the mess from the control-room deck.

It is a good place to compose your thoughts. A man can stand isolated in the bluster of wind and spray while a procession of men ask permission to come up to relieve themselves into the 'pig's ear' before turning in. They stand for a moment, staring out to port, but most are eager to get below again as quickly as possible. Submariners are a strange breed and seem allergic to fresh air, preferring the muggy warmth of the boat.

Solomon requests permission to ditch gash, and soon buckets are being hauled up to the bridge, to be taken aft on to the bandstand, and the contents hurled over the lee rail. Later, when I go through the boat to check all is secure for the night most of the men are already snoring their heads off. In reality the atmosphere inside the submarine remains unchanged, yet in some indefinable way a sense of dusk and nightfall invades the messes, and even the diesels take on a muted tone.

I stand right forward in the torpedo-stowage compartment where the motion is pronounced and my feet leave the deck when the bow drops into a deep trough. The first day is always a shake-down as we change from 'day running' routine to a long cruise. We are still searching for niches to stow away personal items of kit, sorting out our bedding, and adjusting to the comings and goings of the watches. The perpetual rhythm of the diesels resonate through the steel hull as Welks' men watch over them, nursing the thousands of moving parts that grow hot with friction, expanding and contracting hour after hour, day after day. Now they come under even more strain as the tail lifts and dips, one moment gagging the exhausts, and the next raising the screw clear so that it runs wild.

Four days to Gibraltar. A lay-over of twenty-four hours to take on fresh supplies of food and water, then eight days to Port Said across a placid Mediterranean Sea, find us waiting to join a convoy going down through the Suez Canal. A black box is fixed to the fore-part of the casing, with a searchlight and a telephone to the bridge so that the Egyptian lookout can talk to the pilot as we go.

We enter the canal at midnight, and I will share the helm with the gunlayer and Solomon in half-hourly stints, for it is a demanding duty, with no margin for error. The wind that comes down the conning-tower is surprisingly cold, and when I go up top during one of my off-duty spells I find the night air bitter. I look out to port into a violet wilderness of undulating sand-dunes bathed in moonlight bright enough to cast long shadows across the naked waste. It is a petrified ocean that seems to stretch to infinity.

In contrast, when I look to starboard, a million lights twinkle as they reflect in the waterways that run parallel to the canal, and the occasional sweep of car headlights cuts swathes along the tree-lined ribbon of road. Ahead, the canal runs straight as an arrow towards the Bitter Lakes as we lead a long line of merchantmen southward.

I return to the desert on the port side, for there lie the intrigue and mystery that grip my soul. I allow my imagination to paint pictures. Somewhere out there is Bible country with names like Jordan and Sinai. It is a changing world, and I remember sailing up to Akaba where Moslem women still drew water from a well and carried it home on their heads, while camel caravans came in from the desert, and all there was to see on the other side of the strait were two small huts used by an English archaeologist and his son. Now they say a new city is to grow out of the waste called Elat, with modern streets and air-conditioned buildings. The living standards of the Arabs will be improved by all this, and they will live longer and healthier lives. Yet, somehow, when I see the way western dress and values are replacing their traditional ways I feel a great sense of sadness.

I suppose it is all too easy for sentimentalists like me to wax lyrical over a bygone era: I haven't had to suffer the poverty, nor struggle to survive in a land where a man is old at forty. The beauty I see is the cruel beauty that takes no account of living beings. It saps their strength and sucks them dry. Yet I know that there are Arabs who would prefer it to the changes they see taking place.

I shrug those morbid thoughts aside. There is nothing I can do about their problems, and the night is too beautiful to spoil by trying to set the world to rights. Unlike most of my colleagues I cannot rest below and ignore all this. While they snore their heads off in their bunks, completely unaware of this magical panorama sliding past, I am like a big, wide-eyed kid, filled with wonder and speculation as we ride by the fringes of Sinai, and I am loath to miss one second of it.

The sun rises swiftly as we emerge into the open expanse of the Bitter lakes to anchor and wait for the northbound convoy to clear the lower stretch of the canal. We sit in a stagnant pool of blatant heat that bakes the metal and turns the boat into an oven, even though we run out the hoses and damp down the casing to help the air-conditioners keep the temperature down. A flotilla of sailing dinghies comes out to us from the air-bases, loaded with bronzed airmen and squaddies who exchange banter with our blokes as they go swimming over the side.

The first northbound ships sail past in stately procession, dipping their ensigns as they go by. Big, clean Scandinavians with light grey hulls and spotless upperworks. Russians with hammers and sickles on the funnels and women on the bridges, their crews staring back at us with blank faces. Panamanian and Liberian tankers with Lascars and Chinese busy on deck. A cruise liner with hordes of waving tourists lining her rails as they spot our White Ensign; and there is still a fair sprinkling of British freighters amongst them, looking drab alongside the others, with their black hulls and red boot-topping. Their numbers are growing smaller now as many are laid up in remote creeks to queue for the breaker's yard, or change to foreign flags to escape stringent laws and manning restrictions. British seamen who sailed through hell in Atlantic and Russian convoys only six years ago are being put on the beach, or having to scratch about for jobs on cross-Channel ferries to remain at sea.

Suddenly I stiffen. A clan-line freighter is blinking a message from her bridge.

'Thorpe!' I yell down the tower, and the head of an AB looks up at me from below. 'Find Bunts, and tell him to get up here with his aldis at the double!' I shout at him.

The freighter is almost abreast now, and I wave a hand at her, hoping she will realise what is happening and have patience. I search about to see if the lamp has been left up here, but Bunts guards it with his life and has it with him. I must have a go at Tyson about that, for several of us are capable of responding to a merchantman, albeit a lot more slowly than Thorpe, but at least I could have stammered out a brief 'please wait' to hold their attention.

In frustration I go back to the tower. 'Where the hell is that bloody signalman!' I scream at an upturned face.

The face is thrust aside and another takes its place. It is one of the telegraphists, and he comes blundering up the ladder. I step back quickly to allow him past, and he stumbles to the front of the bridge. 'Where's the lamp?' he asks.

'Jesus Christ!' I rave. 'Have you come up without the fucking Aldis?' I look across to where the freighter is slipping away towards the entrance to the northern canal. Her lamp has stopped blinking now, and there is a resentful look to her stern as she runs away from us. A mutual respect exists between the Merchant Service and ourselves, and they expect nothing less than excellence when we meet. I feel a hot flush of shame cross my face as I realise how her officers must feel about being totally ignored by the navy.

The flavour has gone from the day. I shove past the floundering telegraphist and drop down through the hatch. Faces look away when those in the controlroom see the anger on my face, and there is a sudden over-concentration on particular tasks. I go forward past the wardroom and my own mess to the seamen's quarters where a man sits with a bucket between his legs, peeling spuds.

'Where's Bunts?' I ask him.

He shrugs and looks uncomfortable. 'Dunno, Swain.'

I look up and down the passageway. Maybe he is in the

heads: but it is more than ten minutes since I shouted down for him, and that's more than enough time for anyone. I go aft until I come level with the wardroom.

'Anything wrong, Coxswain?' asks Tyson when he sees my red face. He is sitting with the English pilot. Our navigator is pouring the drinks.

'No, sir. I don't think so. I am looking for the signalman, that's all.'

He grins at the others. 'There you are, gentlemen. The case of the missing bunting-tosser. Who we need now is Miss Marple.' He gets a much bigger laugh than he deserves and dries up when he sees my serious face. 'Don't look so concerned, Grant. After all, no one can remain undetected for long in one of these.' He turns away again. 'May I offer you another whisky, pilot?'

I move further aft past the W/T and radar offices into the passageway beyond. The 'chef' is concocting a meal in his minute galley to my right; reminding me that it is well past tot-time and there will be a riot if I don't get round to issuing rum before sailing time. I concentrate on the line of doors to my left. 'Bunts!' I call as I knock on the one that opens into the ratings bathroom. 'Are you there?'

Silence.

I try the door, and it swings ajar to reveal an empty compartment. I stand back with my spine hard against the opposite bulkhead. This is normally a busy thoroughfare, yet no one passes me as I ponder on what to do next, and that is strange in itself. Looking aft, I can see through the bulkhead door into the oily cavern of the engine and motor room where the slumbering diesels glint dully in the artificial light, looking cold and lifeless. A stoker looks up, catches my eye and turns away quickly.

'What the hell is going on?' I mutter aloud. I turn to go through the after bulkhead door, but hesitate when I hear a noise. Remote, secret and indistinct, it comes from the door just forward of the bathroom – the ratings' heads.

'Bunts!' I ask cautiously.

The noise stops. I can almost hear him holding his breath. 'Bunts!' I repeat in a louder voice.

The door swings slowly open and he stands there with his head hanging down. When he looks up I lurch back with a wince. One eye is swollen and shut, and he has a cut lip. The rest of his face is a bloody mess, and when I allow my gaze to wander down over his chest and body I see bruises on his rib-cage and he seems to be having difficulty standing upright.

The signs are obvious, yet how can men come to blows in the confined spaces of a submarine without half the crew knowing all about it? This is not general service, where a couple of men can settle a grudge in some remote corner while lookouts watch for authority. No one fights in submarines without half a dozen seniors jumping in to drag them apart. Whatever has happened here has been done with the full knowledge of at least part of the crew, and with the consent of those who should have put a stop to it at once.

I lean back again. 'All right, Thorpe. What happened to you?'

He eases his body out into the passage; dabbing his mouth with a towel. He tries to reply, but the words don't seem to come easily. He is far worse than I first realised. Reeling all over the place when he tries to stand upright. I reach for him, but he shakes free of my hands to stagger forward into the control-room with me in tow. He fetches up by the diving-panel, and slumps down onto the seat where the trim-pump operator normally sits. Over his shoulder the banks of levers and wheelvalves that flood or blow the main ballast tanks are arrayed like the intricate workings of some weird pipe organ.

He sits for a moment, trying to get his eyes into focus as he stares vacantly up into space. A ripple of laughter comes from the wardroom. I can't keep this secret for long, yet I do not wish to press him. I guess that if I am to learn the truth it must come in his own time. It grieves me to see him like this, for he is a self-possessed, experienced man who has spent most of his service in submarines: one of those extroverts who are always at the centre of things, with a full dialogue of wise-cracks and anecdotes.

'Swain!' Solomon's voice jerks me round. The second coxswain's tone is soft and conspiratorial. 'The lads caught 'im thievin'.'

I straighten up to stare at him in disbelief. A messdeck thief is the lowest form of animal life. A man who cannot keep his hands off his mates' belongings cannot be tolerated on the lower deck where men have to live in close company, and a code of behaviour is essential. When someone breaks that code he brings suspicion on his mates, and the whole system falls apart until the canker is removed.

Once discovered there are two ways of dealing with such a man: official and unofficial. Most men prefer the short sharp unofficial method, even though it is more painful. For the other way leads to enquiries, possible courts martial, and even if he escapes dishonourable discharge, the culprit must carry the stigma for the rest of his service life.

Thorpe knows all this better than most. It just doesn't make sense for a man like him to destroy his future in such a stupid manner. Even in general service it is almost invariably newly enlisted men who thieve, and even then fifty per cent of this type of crime is the result of emotional problems. For an old hand like the leading signalman to rob his mess-mates is unheard of.

'What is he supposed to have stolen?' I ask bluntly.

The second coxswain looks uncomfortable, and his eyes flicker sideways for a moment. 'Two melons – but it isn't as simple as that,' he adds hastily.

'It better not be,' I threaten.

There is a flash of anger in Solomon's eyes. 'We're not that stupid,' he protests in a harsh whisper. He is as desperate as I am to keep this from the wardroom. 'There has been a spate of stealing ever since he came on board, but we have never been able to catch anyone. This time he was caught red-handed; and he admitted taking the melons.'

I swing on Thorpe. 'Well?'

The signalman looks up at me. His expression is defiant. 'I didn't realise those melons belonged to anyone in particular. In my last boat we always kept fresh fruit handy, and we kept it stowed on the bread boards, exactly like it was when I took them. I wouldn't pinch anythin'.'

'The whole thing stinks, Solomon,' I snarl. I am having difficulty keeping my voice down as I seethe with anger. 'Who was responsible for half killing him?'

'He was caught red-handed,' he says lamely.

'So you said,' I sneer. 'Are you trying to tell me that half a dozen blokes just suddenly took it into their heads to beat him up while everyone, including senior hands, just stood about and watched?'

They are both hanging their heads now, unwilling to add anything more.

I turn to Thorpe. 'Why the hell didn't you tell someone you were taking the melons?'

'Jimmy told me I would have to stay on the bridge while we went down the canal, with one of the telegraphists to relieve me if I had to go below. I took one for me and one for him. It was midnight, for Christ sake! I wasn't gonna wake people up just to tell them I was taking two fuckin' melons.' There is a new pleading look in his face when he goes on. 'I've bin in the Andrew eight years. I'm on top line to take my yeoman's course. Do you really think I'd give all that lot up for two poxy melons?'

I study the cortecine deck for a moment. When I ask the next question I want to see the answer in his eyes; not the one he speaks. I jerk my head round and spit the words right into his face. 'Who beat you up?'

His eyes jump towards Solomon.

'Never mind him,' I snarl in a hoarse whisper. 'Look at me when I am talking.'

The moment is gone, though, and he glowers back at me with a belligerent expression on his face. So I switch to Solomon. 'What have you got to say about all this?'

'I didn't see it happen.' Like Thorpe he is a good man, with years of service behind him. That's the way with *Audacity's* company: they are all above average, which makes this business even more incredible.

'If I find out that there is more to this than what you've told me I'll break you, Solomon. I don't have to spell out the penalties for condoning a mess-deck brawl. You could spend the rest of your time in a little round cap.'

He sighs resignedly. 'All right, 'Swain. The truth is that there was a scrap in the after torpedo space. I was comin' out of the heads when I heard the struggle, so I went aft to separate them.'

'Who was fighting?'

He looks away for a second or so. 'I didn't see. Mr Welks was there when I tried to get in amongst them.'

A sudden gust of laughter stills our voices as we wait for it to subside. Thank goodness they're enjoying themselves. The last thing I want is for one of that crowd to come out to see what is going on.

'Mr Welks?' I ask cautiously. 'What was he doing?'

'I dunno. He took me aside and told me to keep my nose out of it and go forward with him. Said it was messdeck justice, and nothing to do with us.'

'Did he now!' Welks has stuck his neck out this time. On the face of it his motives might be all right, but I doubt it. Welks has never gone out of his way to promote good relations with his crowd, and I can't see him changing now. He seems to thrive on oppression, quick to clamp down on anyone who so much as looks like being insubordinate. That is what makes him such an odd-ball in boats, and why I get so mad when I see him still serving in them.

'Do you really believe that you are going to get away with this when they see the state of your face, Thorpe?' I ask sardonically. 'What will you tell Tyson?'

'I'll say I got tangled up in a fight in Port Said. It was dark on the bridge last night, so I doubt if anyone really got a good look at me. They ain't gonna question it.'

I turn to Solomon. 'And you think that will be an end to it, do you?'

He shrugs. 'You ain't gonna make a fuss, are you, Bunts?'

The signalman looks away. 'Why should I? I know when I'm bloody well licked.'

That puts it down to me. These two will stick together like glue. I look from one to the other, knowing that I represent authority, and it puts me on the other side of the fence. 'Well I'm not satisfied.' I declare grimly. 'If I get so much as a sniff of anything like this again, I'll crucify you.'

I leave them standing looking after me as I go back to my mess, where I sit with a mug of tea clasped in my hands, contemplating the table-top. Deep down I know this is not the end; not by a long chalk, but if I make an issue of it I will stir up so much muck it could disrupt the whole boat. Rightly or wrongly I decide to sit on it.

We leave the canal astern to go south down the Red Sea with both shores pulling back on either side. It will take time for Thorpe to re-establish himself, even though everyone makes an effort to forgive and forget now that he has been punished. He withdraws into his own little world, burying his old extroverted image beneath a cloak of resentment, a lonely man in a closeknit community of sixty blokes.

'Signalman to the bridge!' is no longer a cue for a tirade of sham abuse and good-natured banter. In a narrow seaway like this there is a constant stream of ships passing or overtaking us, and the skipper insists on talking to most of them – especially the British ones. If the officers notice the change in Thorpe they make no mention of it, and by the time we are shaping up for Aden his attitude is accepted by most as the norm. I seem to be the only one conscious of the effect he is having on the boat. So much so, I stick my neck out and suggest to Tyson that an extra day in port to allow the men to get ashore before the long leg to Singapore wouldn't go amiss.

Give him his due, he takes my request to heart and has a quiet word with the skipper, but the response is anything but quiet. The skipper seems to take the suggestion as a personal affront, and the whole boat hears him condemn their first lieutenant for daring to even think about delaying our journey out to the war-zone. One phrase registers above all others in my mind when I listen to him rave. 'Do you want us to miss the bloody war for the sake of a run ashore, Number One?'

No one broaches the subject again and we swelter in the heat of the port while we take on stores from lighters as we lie alongside a water-tender. It is like a furnace on the casing as the sun reflects off the deep blue water, where dhows and other small craft weave crazy courses between huge merchantmen with no regard for 'rules-of-the-road.' Lumbering freighters blow angry blasts on their sirens to clear the way and reach moorings, where hoards of natives with jet-black faces swarm on board to toil in gangs while brutal supervisors bully them on to stagger about with impossible loads on their shoulders.

The edge of the tide is lined with rows of flat-roofed buildings; open doored and windowless, spilling tables and goods out onto the pavements. Above them dun-coloured hills rise majestically in forbidding ramparts to deter the foolhardy from venturing into the arid hell of the desert that lies beyond. On high ground to the right of the town a cluster of more opulent buildings squat, where the privileged can sit in relative coolness beneath rotating fans, sipping long drinks served by unobtrusive waiters, aloof from the sweaty turmoil that goes on below.

I am one of the fortunate who manage to get ashore to buy fresh fruit and vegetables, and I manage to persuade Tyson to let Hancock come with me. Our taxi-driver tells us about his three wives and how to keep from getting our throats cut while we search through the market. By the time we return and hire a boat to take us out to the boat we are both heartily sick of the place. When all is considered, perhaps the men haven't missed much, though I doubt if anyone could persuade them of that.

Much of the time is spent catching up with personal chores. Dhobying our kit and taking showers while there is plenty of fresh water available. When we sail the ratings' bathroom will be out of bounds again, stacked up with an overflow of stores, restrictions will be put on the use of water.

During our journey down through the Red Sea some clever dick realised that the air-conditioners were producing about a ton of uncontaminated water each day, so we rigged a pump and hose into the periscope well to provide a reservoir of dubious liquid for anyone who felt desperate enough to lower a bucket. The effort involved, and the fact that when you finished washing yourself down you wound up smellier than when you started discouraged all except the most fastidious.

Ahead lies the longest leg of our journey. The captain refuses to entertain any ideas of calling into Trincomalee to break the four thousand miles trip. So, using number four ballast tank for extra fuel, we take on fifty-five thousand gallons to give us a range of over ten thousand miles at eleven knots, but eleven knots is not enough for our impatient captain, who wants to maintain a steady fifteen in order to complete the crossing in ten days, and that increases consumption considerably.

It isn't much of an ordeal by wartime standards, and *Audacity*, with her air-conditioning and superior living standards should take it in her stride. However, the men have already spent almost twenty days at sea with two limited stops, and cannot see a reason for not being allowed on shore, even for a short break. Therefore it is a disgruntled crew that puts to sea after their short stay at Aden. The adrenalin that flows through a man when he is on wartime patrol is missing. Long periods of boredom are welcomed under those conditions, for the alternative is moments of sheer terror when all hell breaks loose and the enemy is out to blast you into oblivion.

No one moans about lack of excitement in those

circumstances, but now everyone knows that we are being driven on by a man who is hungry for glory. After five years of 'real' war the experienced men in the boat can hardly take this Korean thing seriously. It has the smell of a local conflict about it, and it poses no threat to the folk back home. It niggles the crew, and their respect for Studding and his over-enthusiasm wanes.

Tyson and I get our heads together and organise inter-branch 'ucker' tournaments, talent competitions, tombola, and even persuade the captain to allow swimming over the side each evening. We have a movie projector and half a dozen films which are rationed out to one performance every second day to make them last. This, along with a selection of recorded radio programmes and music, helps to keep us sane throughout the endless days when the horizon stays blank, and we sail under a canopy of washed-out blue.

Two days out salt water contaminates one of the electrical distillers, and the other one breaks down in sympathy, so water is rationed. The atmosphere and temper inside the boat grows less sweet by the hour. Only the weather remains monotonously placid, each day a carbon copy of the one before, with the same interminable circle of bland sea surrounding us. It is as though a giant magnet holds us in the centre of our own patch of ocean.

Now and again a ship goes by, and Thorpe clacks out a greeting, followed by the standard 'what ship – where bound.' Some respond with enthusiasm, while others reluctantly dip their ensigns, spell out the barest details, then lapse into a stolid silence.

The daily swimming sessions are tolerated with growing impatience by the skipper. He never indulges himself, but prefers to drum his fingers on the bridge rail as he watches the minute hand of his watch creep round until he can blow his whistle to 'clear the water.' The diesels thunder into life almost before the last man has climbed out of the water.

For me there are magic moments. Times when shoals of

flying fish skit across the sparkling surface with flashes of silver, and I try to forget that they are not doing it for sheer pleasure, but because some unspeakable predator lurks under their vulnerable bellies. Times when the sky is filled with stars so bright I feel I can reach out and touch them, and the moon spreads a path of shimmering light across the ocean as we plough along.

I have plenty of opportunity, for I am hauled in to help with the bridge watches. By tradition Tyson takes the morning watch, so I volunteer to take the 'last dog' and 'middle' to allow the navigator and Subby to share the daytime spells and be available to the skipper when needed. It leaves me free to do my paperwork during the forenoon when the crew turn to for work, and to crash out in my bunk during the afternoon.

Sometimes, when the lookouts and I are isolated in our small world while the rest of the boat slumbers we feel we have to hold our breath as the magnificence of a tropical night takes hold and dwarfs us into insignificance. At such times it is hard to force Zoe from my mind. Two letters caught up with me at Aden, querulous, apologetic, and talking as though this is only a postponement to our plans. A dozen times I sit down to reply, but there is always a bustle going on, and nowhere to assemble my thoughts and put them into words while I sit cheek to jowl with my messmates.

In those crystal nights when even the wind seems to hold its breath the ache grips with a cruel force. This is no fairy-tale romance. It is an all-consuming yearning to spend the rest of my life with her. She is part of the picture that forms in my mind when I think of my future, far away from this metallic, impersonal world, with curtains and a fireside, where a man can sit in blessed silence and the room stays absolutely still.

'Do you think men will ever get to stand on the moon?'

Subby's voice cuts into my thoughts. He is the last thing I need at this moment. 'Sir?'

'The moon,' he repeats, nodding towards the big candlewax disc that floats amongst the stars. 'They say it won't be long before someone tries to send a rocket up there.'

'Not in my lifetime,' I declare tersely. His public school manner, and boyish enthusiasm niggles me. He's a decent youngster, but a pain in the arse for a lot of us.

'Why are you so certain?' he asks, warming to his subject.

I sigh heavily, wanting desperately to be rid of him. 'Because it is about three hundred and sixty thousand miles away and travelling at a hell of a speed. You know how long air lasts in one of these boats: even if they could work out the statistics it would take days to get there; land and take off again, then come all the way back. Try working that lot out on the "fruit machine".'

He stays silent for a moment. 'You married, Grant?'

I deliberately turn my back on him to stare out at an imaginary object with my binoculars. 'No, sir.'

'Not interested?' he persists, moving closer. He has a skin like a bloody rhino, 'In settling down, I mean.'

'Haven't thought about it.'

'That's strange, I would have thought that you of all people would know exactly where you are going.'

I smirk. 'It ain't always that easy, sir.'

'No,' he says with an edge to his voice. 'It isn't, is it? I wish I knew more about myself sometimes. I imagine you to be a very masculine man, Grant.'

I snap a look at him. 'What kind of a question is that?'

He jumps back. 'Oh, I didn't mean to offend you. It – it's just that sometimes I feel a bit lost, as though I don't fit in with the others in the wardroom.'

I'm getting sick of this. 'It'll come, sir. Now, don't you think you should get below and get some shut-eye?'

At last he gets the message and slopes off below to his bunk. I heave a sigh of relief and try, without success, to regain my thoughts about Zoe. Perhaps it is just as well, for a man cannot function properly if half his mind is on other things, yet I curse Subby for making a bloody nuisance of himself: I have enough on my plate without having to wet-nurse him.

By morning the air-conditioners are giving trouble, adding to our discomfort as the humidity rises. Already I have treated two cases of prickly heat, and with water rationed there is a constant worry about dehydration. It is the age-old submarine problem, and although we cut down clothing to the bare essentials the sweat oozes out of our pores and dirt clings to our skin, until our bodies stink. Each time I climb down into the boat from the fresh air on the bridge the sour taste clogs my throat until I become adjusted to it once more.

Inevitably the complaints come. The engine-room brigade is the main target, for they are held responsible for the distillers and air-conditioners going out of action. Interbranch banter hardens to snide comments that are more and more difficult to shrug off. Many of Welks's men do not see daylight as often as the seamen, and stand their watches in the clamorous, oily confines of the engine-room. They resent the sarcastic remarks of the dabtoes, and a rift develops between both sides that did not exist before.

In the torrid atmosphere tempers grow ever shorter, and senior hands need to be on their guard against sudden eruptions. They have to step in quickly at times to separate hot-heads when they threaten to tear each other apart. Only one man seems oblivious to what is going on. Welks takes no part in our efforts to relieve boredom. He drives his men without mercy. Blames their incompetence for the shortcomings of the equipment, and refuses to accept any responsibility himself. Always carping, his men get to detest the sound of his nasal voice.

Everyone knows what the crew needs. Studding has driven us on with only three short stops at Gib, Port Said, and Aden, that served only to increase our yearning to set foot on land for a while, and scrub the filth from our bodies and clothing. Everyone knows that Trinco lies only a day away to the north, yet we press on for another two thousand miles because of the captain's obsession with getting into the fight.

The men are stale and resentful. This specially selected crowd who once backed their skipper to the hilt is beginning to have doubts about his motives. The well-oiled teamwork that he built up with endless drills is breaking down, and because the standards set in *Audacity* are so high it is even more noticeable.

We are beginning to run out of ideas to keep the men occupied, and there seems nothing to do but allow things to go on as they are and hope for the best. There is talk of introducing evolutions and drill, but as this would inevitably include diving the skipper refuses to entertain the idea. Even if we use the snort-mast our speed will be cut down, and his criterion is to reach the war-zone at the earliest possible moment.

A new crisis is developing too. Each news broadcast brings added concern, for the North Koreans have driven south until they are pushing against a small perimeter round the port of Pusan, and there is every possibility that some sort of compromise will have to be reached with the communists before we arrive.

So we sweat it out. Hour after hour the diesels thunder away at full speed, with one day merging into the next with mind-numbing repetition. The taste goes out of the food and our bodies reek with congealed dirt. Nothing breaks the awful monotony of that slummy atmosphere.

IV

An animal-like growl is the first indication I get that something is happening in the fore-ends. I exchange a brief look with my colleagues before we join in a concerted rush, tumbling forward to the small hatch that opens into the torpedo-stowage compartment where a full-blown battle is in progress.

Fists and boots are flying, and the men are tearing into each other in a strange muted mêlée, as if they are deliberately keeping the noise down to keep their conflict to themselves. The lack of sound makes it all the more awesome. Only the muffled grunts and heavy breathing emanates from the turmoil as they launch into one another with terrible dedication.

When I thrust my body into the mass to try to drag them apart wild-eyed sailors turn on me and lash out at my face in a mindless fury, willing to hit out at anything that moves. I feel a kind of insanity building inside me too – a sort of relief as I retaliate. There is an overwhelming satisfaction in striking someone and feeling your fist sink into soft flesh. It is made even more incredible by the lack of shouting and screaming. All we need to do is work the tension out of ourselves, and I realise that I am actually enjoying it.

With an effort I regain my senses, and with a great deal of effort, bring myself under control. I am caught up in the midst of it, and I have to fight to save myself from injury, but at least I know what I'm about. My shouts and threats go unheeded as the battle surges from side to side. I recognise leading hands and petty officers who should be helping to restore order grinning all over their stupid faces as they join in. It is as if every blow brings infinite relief, like a huge safety valve. Whatever started the affray is long forgotten, and there is no real viciousness. It is like an overblown pillow-fight for adults.

It hardly requires the blast of Tyson's whistle to stop it, for the sweltering heat has taken its toll and drained the energies out of most of them. They slump back to look at each other with silly grins all over their faces, pointing at bloody noses and eyes that are puffed and closing. Stokers and seamen start to giggle like kids, wallowing in their own mess while they scramble up to their feet and take stock of themselves.

I catch Hancock grinning at me from the other side of the crowd. Someone makes a ribald comment and brings a roar of laughter from his mates. They are helping each other up, no longer partisan as they probe about for remote injuries. 'Get yer fat arse aht of me face, Guns!' protests a voice from the depths, and a new burst of laughter roars out.

For a moment I believe a new sanity is being restored, and this surge of spontaneous relief will sustain us until we reach Singapore. Whatever the rights and wrongs of it the men are closer to normality than they have been for many days. I glance over at the first lieutenant and see his anger dissolving as he realises what I do. No harm has been done, except for a few split lips and black eyes. His eyes catch mine, and for one cautionary moment we look at each other, knowing there is no excuse for mess-deck brawls, and that the senior hands should have known better, but then I see his expression ease, and we grin to each other. On this occasion it is wise to bend the rules.

'I'll see you in the controlroom with Petty Officer Hancock, Grant,' he states firmly, and even this half-serious threat brings a laugh from the crowd as he turns away.

'Get this bloody mess cleared up!' I yell at them, before I tumble through the hatch after him.

Inside the controlroom the draught is being sucked down like a gale, and the helmsman is having an easy time holding course in a flat calm sea.

'What happened forward, Hancock?' asks Tyson.

The TGM bites his lips thoughtfully. 'I didn't see the start of it, sir. I was down amongst number five and six tubes when it began, and by the time I got my head up the scrap was in full swing.'

'You should have tried to stop it.'

Hancock gasps at the thought. 'It would have bin like tryin' to stop a bloody hurricane, sir.'

Tyson looks at me. 'There were leading hands, Grant. How did it get out of hand like that? We cannot put up with this sort of thing. What the hell were they thinking of?'

I shrug. 'Maybe, like me, they thought it was just a bit of a rough and tumble; not to be taken too seriously. After all, no one got hurt, and I think that they got something out of their systems.'

'I wish I could believe that.'

I press my point while he is on the run. 'Some blokes got a bit carried away, but it was a good-natured affair for the most part.' I can see his thoughts ticking over. 'If I could make a suggestion, sir.'

'Go ahead.'

'Things will only get worse if we put some of the men in the rattle. It will mean that their leave will be stopped at Singapore, and that will tighten the atmosphere even more. Extra work will do it. Get them turned to in the dog-watches and suspend the film shows for those who took part. That should do it.'

'Hm!' He runs the implications through his mind. 'I'll have to make some kind of report to the captain. He is bound to know that something went on, especially when he sees the cuts and bruises.'

'The cork had to pop sometime, sir. They've got it out of their systems now. Relations between the deck crowd and the engine-room were at rock bottom. I think we should be grateful that it wasn't a lot more serious. Let's face it, sir: I've seen rougher rugby scrums.'

He nods. 'What would you describe it as, a fight, a brawl, or just a good-natured rough and tumble?'

Before I can reply Hancock steps in. 'I saw most of it, sir. I would call it horse-play – nothing more.'

Tyson stares into space. There is no more advice we can give. When it all comes down to it he is the one who must take the can. If he condones what's happened it could undermine discipline, and he could face a charge of neglecting his duty. On the other hand, if he makes a big issue of it the whole company will be disrupted, and the boat will take a long time to recover. Studding's reputation will be at stake, and we might even miss the war while extensive enquiries are held.

'We will stop their rum and suspend the film shows for everyone. That will affect the innocent as well as the guilty, and teach everyone that such behaviour will not be tolerated.' His face hardens. 'However, if anyone steps out of line from now on I will come down on him like a ton of bricks, and the onus will be on senior hands to take the full weight – is that clear?'

Hancock and I reply in unison. He leaves us standing there while he goes off to make his report to the captain.

'Thank Gawd for one thing,' breathes Hancock as Tyson's feet disappear through the lower hatch.

'Wassat?'

'It happened before and not after tot time.'

When I turn to go forward I run smack into Welks. He is standing squarely in front of me with an inimical look on his face. 'So it is to be another bloody whitewash is it, Grant?'

'That is up to the first lieutenant, sir.' I stare him straight in the eye. 'No good making a mountain out of a molehill, as they say.'

'It was a full-scale riot, and you know it.'

This is as close as we have come to each other since he joined the boat. The one good thing about his commission is that he lives in a separate mess, and we can stay well apart for most of the time. He has gained weight since Norway, and there is an unhealthy pallor in his bloated features, but that same expression of contempt is ever present, along with his weasel eyes and sneering mouth. No man is responsible for his looks, but I am more than half convinced that Welks goes out of his way to cultivate his evil countenance.

'Still overstepping your authority, Grant?' he snipes. 'Taking it upon yourself to make the rules as you go along to toady your mates at the expense of my stokers?'

I can sense Hancock fidgeting behind me. He cannot know what has gone on between us in the past, but anyone with half an eye can see what effect Welks is having on the boat, and the TGM is not likely to desert me now.

'A coxswain is supposed to be impartial, Grant,' persists Welks. 'Shielding your own kind is out of order.'

I am struggling to keep my feelings under control, but it is difficult with his foul breath souring my nostrils. 'I don't know what you are implying, sir.'

'I've got a leading stoker with a broken wrist, and another with a suspected cracked rib. Both of them are unfit for duty, and both received their injuries at the hands of your hooligans. What have you to say about that?'

I sigh heavily. 'That's news to me, sir. Why didn't you mention it before, sir. You must have heard most of what was being said between the first lieutenant and myself, sir?'

He is seething. 'Don't tell me what I should and shouldn't do!' he explodes. 'You were in so quick to protect your lot, no one had time to tell anyone anything.'

'That ain't so!' blurts out Hancock vigorously. 'We didn't know anyone was hurt.'

'Keep out of this and get on with your duties!' roars Welks.

'Not before I have had my say.' Hancock is not a man to back down when he thinks he is in the right. He is sticking his neck out for me as he confronts the engineer. 'I was there long before Grant arrived. It was a mess-deck rumpus that would have fizzled out on its own. Your blokes got hurt by accident.'

'I won't tell you again, Hancock. Get forward to where you belong.'

I place a steadying hand on the TGM's sleeve and nod towards the bulkhead door. I can feel his body shaking, but he has gone far enough, and I cannot let him get into real trouble. He gives me a sideways look before shuffling away, muttering, none too quietly, about 'jumped-up warrant officers who act like bloody ODs.'

I am amazed that Welks doesn't call him back and lay into him for his insubordination, but at the moment I am his prime target.

'I am going to speak to the captain, Grant. You have gone too far this time, and you haven't got a group of your croneys to back you up. One thing you should know is that one of my men owned a threepenny bit that was given to him when he was christened; kept inside a leather wallet with other personal items. They were found with other stolen goodies spilling out of a moneybelt belonging to the signalman. Do you still believe him to be innocent?'

'I'm not committing myself either way, sir.'

'No,' he breathes sarcastically, 'you wouldn't. Well, you can't whitewash this, Grant. I think the captain should know what's going on, don't you?'

'May I remind you – sir. You stood by while Thorpe got duffed up by his mates. Are you going to see him punished twice?'

He bites his lip. 'You know damned well why I did that. We try to stay out of domestic problems. He hasn't learned his lesson though, has he? Now I have no option, and you're not coming out this smelling of roses either. Your lax attitude is mainly responsible for what happened, and I'll see that you get what's coming to you. It has taken a long time, Grant, but you are due for a well-earned come-down.'

He is breathing heavily, red-faced and pop-eyed, as though he is about to explode. His body stinks with more than sweat while he slavers over his words. I would say that he is a bundle of nerves, and I can't believe that I am responsible for him getting worked up into this state. There is nothing more I can say while he is raving like this, so I do the only thing possible: turn my back on him, and deliberately walk away, leaving him clenching and unclenching his fists as he watches me go.

By the time I have examined the two injured men Welks has made his report to the skipper. When I get to the bridge the atmosphere is taut. Studding is having difficulty keeping his feelings in check, and he listens tight-lipped while I explain that I have bound up the man with the injured chest.

'The leading stoker is another matter, sir,' I go on quietly. 'His wrist is a mess. He can't move his fingers, and the injury is inflamed and swollen. He is in a lot of pain.'

He grips the fore-part of the bridge and stares out to sea while Tyson spells out two alternatives for getting the man to medical aid. 'We can ask the Indians to fly him ashore in a Sunderland flying boat, or we can divert to make a rendezvous with *Neptune* who is exercising her aircraft one hundred miles to the south of our present position. She's faster than us, but she has made longer stop-overs at Malta and Aden, so we are running more or less neck and neck.'

The skipper swings on him with blazing eyes. 'Is that meant to be a statement, Tyson? Damn it, man! Can't you control the ship's company? Am I to be plagued with people who are determined to set every obstacle in my way?'

The first lieutenant swallows hard as he gulps back an angry retort. Like me he knows that this would not have occurred if the men had been given a decent run ashore. 'I don't think anyone could have foreseen this, sir,' he says drily.

'You think not? By what Mr Welks tell me, a full-scale riot broke out in the fore-ends and we have a bloody thief in the boat! Yet, no one seems to have done a damn thing about it. Christ, Andy! Don't you realise that every hour is precious on this trip?'

'It was nothing like a riot, sir. It was a rough and tumble, that's all. The injuries were unfortunate, but they should add only one day to our schedule.'

'Oh no they won't, Number One,' grinds Studding grimly. 'Not one minute will be added to our programme, I'll see to that. Even if it means curtailing shore-leave at Singapore.' He slams his hand down on the wooden capping. 'They have brought this on themselves, and deserve all they get for behaving like a lot of demented hooligans.'

Tyson sucks in his breath and exchanges looks with me, but decides not to challenge that for the moment. 'What is it to be, sir?' he asks evenly, 'The Sunderland or *Neptune*?'

'*Neptune*. I am not crawling to the Indians. Tell Pilot to work out a course, and get a signal off to the carrier with full details.' He sighs heavily and drops his tone. 'You know, Andy. The Americans would use a helicopter for this, and there would be hardly a hiccup in our schedule. If our lords and masters did not have their heads buried in the past our man could be picked up and flown to the carrier in a couple of hours. Instead, it is going to take all day just to reach her, let alone transfer him.'

'Yes, sir.'

'Get on with it then, and let's hope *Neptune* is where she is supposed to be. Perhaps we can do it without losing more than a few hours.'

He is over-optimistic. His counterpart in *Neptune* leaps at an opportunity to use *Audacity* as a clockwork mouse for his airmen to have a go at. He ignores Studding's protests and insists on carrying out a full-scale exercise, including a submerged attack, after the injured man has been transferred.

The skipper seethes as we forge ahead of the carrier to make our dive and begin a long-winded approach. First we use the snort to gain an attacking position, then we creep in on an intercepting course with Studding fuming at the periscope. Everyone learns to stay well away from him as he frets and curses. In the end we lose three whole days before *Neptune's* captain decides he has had enough, signals his thanks and presents his backside to us to go surging off at full speed for Singapore.

Now things really tighten up. Swimming is suspended, and Welks is told to get his finger out and push up our speed. We sweat and gripe our way eastwards, and the niggling starts again. The safety valve that released pent-up emotions has shot its bolt, and nerves are jumping as the skipper keeps up the pressure. Tyson and I put off until the very last minute the awful moment when we must approach him with yet another delaying problem.

'Are you going to arrange with HMS *Terror* for an enquiry, sir?' asks the first lieutenant.

'Enquiry!' he thunders, as though the word is blasphemous.

I stand well back, clutching a written statement of what took place in the fore-ends. If it was not for the debilitating injuries to the two stokers the whole thing could be treated internally, but even Studding cannot ignore a formal accusation from Welks, who still insists that his men were deliberately attacked, and those who should have done something about it just stood by and allowed it to happen. He seems determined to have the whole thing sorted out in Singapore. With the prospect of a further delay, and the need to find a replacement for Thorpe, if he persists in adding the charge of stealing to his list.

Studding glowers at Tyson. 'I hold you largely responsible for this mess, Number One. You and the coxswain should have had your fingers on the pulse. The war in Korea is already a month old, and there is every sign that some sort of deal will be worked out before we get a sniff of the action. We would have the chance to show those penny-pinching politicians at home the true value of retaining a strong submarine service at a time when they are more inclined to restore old, clapped-out boats than thinking of building new ones. Send Welks to me, I'll soon put a stop to his bloody nonsense.'

Tyson is determined to have everything out in the open

now. 'Are you forgetting the repairs to the air-conditioner and the distilling plant, sir? We need specialists to put them right.'

'No I haven't forgotten,' blares the skipper. 'I intend to radio ahead and suggest that the units are examined and assessed by artificers en-route to Hong Kong if necessary. Any spare parts required can be flown on ahead – to Japan if needs be. I am determined to make up lost time, Number One. I will also request recreational facilities to be made available at Terror for our men to get cleaned and exercised. Provided there are no more unfortunate incidents we should cut our turn-round to a minimum.'

'And what about shore-leave, sir?' asks Tyson, carefully avoiding my eyes.

Studding looks away with an impatient toss of his head. 'There is a war going on. I will make up my mind about shore-leave when and if the appropriate opportunity comes. Leave is a privilege – it has to be earned.'

'Yes, sir.' We watch him disappear through the upper hatch.

A deep gloom settles throughout the boat. The men seem to sense that there is a threat to their long-awaited shore-leave, but no one really believes it will be denied them. That would be utterly unthinkable after more than a month at sea, and anyone who suggests such a thing is immediately shouted down. Their feelings are reflected in their faces when they take note of their captain's morose expression, and the way he drums his fingers as he stands on the bridge, staring at the horizon, willing the boat on to its destination. He says little, and treats everyone with suspicion.

I am concerned about Thorpe, for he is living a nightmare. Deep down I can't believe he is guilty. He is by no means a stupid man, and knows full well that he faces ruin, but when I try to get through to him my words are met with resentful monosyllables. He seems to have lost the will to protest his innocence even though his future is on the line.

He wraps himself in a cocoon, hurt and angry at the way his ship-mates have turned against him.

When his duties take him up to the bridge he is coldly efficient, rattling out signals to other ships with a deadpan expression on his face, and using the bare minimum of words to convey messages or respond to orders. Otherwise he maintains a brooding silence that unnerves everyone.

Attempts are made to drag him out of his morbidness by his more discerning mates, but he rejects them all, until inevitably they give up and shrug him off. I tell him to pull himself together and that he will get a full, unbiased hearing, but it is like talking to a dead man, and in the end even my patience is exhausted. So he is left to stew in his own juice, and wallow in his own misery. Guilty or not, Thorpe is condemning himself, and there is nothing to be done about it as far as I can see.

The endless circle of nothingness gives way one morning to the first lush greenery of an island with luxuriant cascades of tropical forest tumbling in profusion to the waterline. Twigs and branches drift past the hull as we approach the land, and a sweet, pungent smell of jungle comes out to us as we sail by. It is sucked down into the hull to merge with the oily, man-made stink in a sickly cocktail as we enter the Straits of Malacca, with Malaya to port and Sumatra to starboard.

Eventually we are surrounded by islands; each more lush than the last, and the radar picks up the big reflectors from the buoyed channel that takes us round the back of Singapore island to the dockyard, for the navy goes in by the back door. I miss the final stages for I have to take the helm and try to ignore the fragrant aromas that come down the conning-tower on the forced draught of the diesels. Up top they are watching a kaleidoscope of exotic vegetation slip by. 'God, Zoe!' I think to myself. 'What would I not give to share some of this with you!'

We berth alongside *Neptune,* with a couple of pontoons to protect her side, and no sooner are we secured than a stream of people cross the plank and descend into the boat to get to grips with our machinery. They wrinkle their noses when they get their first whiff of the interior, and with all hatches open our engines rumble to provide a through draught while they top up the batteries and improve the atmosphere. It takes time to clear away the acrid stench of stale sweat, sour vegetables and hot oil.

First man ashore is the captain, who goes striding off to a waiting jeep, clutching a leather briefcase that bulges with papers. He is on his way to the administration block of HMS *Terror*. By mid-morning we are settled into harbour routine and the first bunch of men are on their way to take advantage of the shore-base facilities to scrub the ingrained filth from their bodies and launder their clothes. Tot-time is a lively affair today. Those who have been to Singapore before respond eagerly to questions from their mates, and everyone is anxious to sample the delights of the port.

To make things worse *Neptune's* loud-speakers relay warnings to her libertymen about avoiding dark alleyways, and being enticed away from their mates by trishawmen and prostitutes, for they are just as likely to get their throats cut as contract VD. There is an element on shore who are impatient to be rid of the last vestige of British domination, and angry at the time it is taking to happen.

Every since Sir Thomas Raffles 'acquired' the 'Lion City' on behalf of the East India Company the British seem to have gone out of their way to alienate the Singaporeans with mindless extravagance and an insensitive attitude to the natives – right up to the last moment, when the Japs confounded all the experts by advancing south through the jungle, and paddling across the straits in collapsible boats. In spite of being outnumbered three to one by the garrison they took the island and renamed it Syonan – 'Land of the South' – and might have earned respect for their military prowess if they had not followed it up with a regime of bestiality. Signs of their occupation are still to be seen on shore, though whether our lads will get to see them is questionable.

Regardless of all this there is an air of optimistic excitement in the boat as the men sweat themselves into a lather in their efforts to get the work done so that they will be ready to go the moment the call for libertymen comes; I haven't the guts to tell them they may not get ashore, mainly because I cannot believe it myself.

Those who work on the casing watch for the first sign of the captain returning, and tense in anticipation when they see his long body descend the ladder from *Neptune's* high flank. He wears an expression we have not seen for many days and even flashes a wide grin at Subby, who calls the men to attention and gives an awkward salute.

'The skipper's back!'

The word spreads through the boat in record time. You can almost taste the tension as the minutes tick by. A half hour, then a full hour, with precious periods of shore-leave time ebbing away. The cleaning is done, and they are going through the motions of polishing brasswork, yet still no word comes from the wardroom. I feel eyes following me about, for the coxswain is always 'in the know' regarding leave, and they are convinced that I am keeping it to myself.

Studding must know the effect his silence is having, yet he drags it out until both watches have eaten in the barracks. I have never seen meals eaten so quickly, nor with less appetite. The officers, including the captain, are invited to dine in *Neptune,* and it is two o'clock before they return to the boat. What I read in Tyson's face doesn't please me, and he goes out of his way to avoid my eyes.

At three o'clock, when tension is almost at breaking point the tannoy crackles into life and a metallic voice announces. 'This is the captain!' and the silence comes like a clap of thunder.

'We have come a long way to fight a war,' the disembodied voice intones. 'And for a while it looked as though we were going to be done out of playing our part, for there is little scope for submarines in Korean waters apparently. They had us down to join the China Fleet in its mundane exercises with anti-submarine units of the Australian Navy.'

He allows his words to sink in before he draws breath and goes on in lighter vein. 'You will be glad to learn that we are not to be left out of the conflict. There is a mission for *Audacity*, for which she is most suited. I cannot tell you more about it now, but I will say that it is an independent scheme of great strategic importance, and I have been to great lengths convincing our lords and masters that we are the ones for the job. I know you will not expect any jingoistic nonsense from me, so I'll get straight to the point. We are a supremely trained unit, and I know that none of you wish to see all that go to waste. Therefore, I have promised that we can achieve a turn-round – if necessary by working shifts overnight – and be ready for sea by oh eight double oh tomorrow. The air-conditioners will have to wait, but we may be able to repair the distillation plant on the way to Hong Kong.

'I promise you that each watch will get a run ashore when we dock there, and of course there will be other opportunities to take in the dubious delights of Singapore. Right now we have more urgent commitments.'

His final words fall on our ears like lead, and the tannoy clicks off to leave a stunned silence. Something hits the pressure-hull and scrapes along the skin with the current. It is the only sound as we nurse our disbelief. In the fore-ends a man is poised with an electric iron; frozen in the act of pressing his shore-going togs. He is like a statue for a moment as he absorbs the words. It looks as if he is about to fling the iron across the compartment, but in the end he resumes his pressing, carefully folding the garments before stowing them away.

There is nothing to be said. This bombshell is beyond the scope of normal lower-deck 'drips.' I snap out of my stupor and gaze about me at the grim faces. 'Right then!' I bark, with more conviction than I feel. 'You heard what the captain said. The casing-party may as well get up top and make ready for shifting berth to go alongside the jetty. The rest of you stow away loose gear and make room for the stores. The sooner we get on with it the better.'

Nothing – not even a reproachful look. They watch my face with dead eyes as I turn away, for I cannot meet those eyes any more. There is a gradual stirring in the boat, and I feel a need for a breath of fresh air. I climb the ladder to the bridge and stare out across the strait at the greenery. It looks less inviting now. A twisted mass of humid jungle that hides a diseased squallor that stifles and rots with its foul breath. The scent is sickly now, heavy in the stagnant air, and there is menace in the dark avenues that lead inland.

The sun is trapped in this basin, and the slow-moving current moves a sludge past the hull in a glutinous soup, with broken foliage and dockyard scum giving it body. Behind me the brittle, rattling noise of the wharf grates on my nerves, and I curse the place for its hidden menace. A body slumps into the space beside me as Hancock rests his elbows on the hot metal and looks out with his cap pushed back on his greying hair.

'I never would have believed it,' he muses softly. 'He had the whole crew on his side a short while ago. Now he's thrown it all down the scuppers for a capful of glory.'

I can't find an answer. We are out of earshot, so anything he says stays with us, and he is only expressing my own thoughts, so there is no point in warning him to watch his words.

'As though another twenty-four hours could make any difference,' he goes on bitterly. 'Just one run ashore would have got the stink of the boat out of their systems and put them on his side. They would follow him to the moon if he played square with them. Now he has missed his chance and soured the boat. They won't forgive him this.'

I still make no answer: Pushing myself away to leave him on his own, still staring out across the water as I ease my body through the upper hatch to slowly climb down into the control-room where the navigator and Tyson are studying charts and discussing the next stage of our journey.

'Excuse me, sir.'

'What is it, Grant?' Tyson rolls over onto one elbow to look at me.

'Leading Signalman Thorpe, sir. What about him?'

He stretches his body as upright as possible beneath the rounded deckhead. Rolls his pencil between his fingers, and contemplates it thoughtfully. 'I have spoken to the captain and he has decided to let it rest for the time being. There is no chance of a replacement before tomorrow, so we shall just have to keep an eye on him.' He looks up at me. 'That will be your province, Grant. In effect, he will be under open arrest.'

I glance at the navigator who has suddenly become totally absorbed in his charts. I realise then that they must have been discussing the captain's decision, for there isn't a pencil mark on the chart.

'We are ready to shift berth, sir,' I state laconically.

'Right. I shall be up in a moment. It's only a shunt, so we won't go to full harbour stations.'

'Subby's got the watch, sir. It might be an idea to let him do it,' suggests the navigator.

Tyson looks away. 'It's a nice thought, Pilot, and it does you credit. However, all we need to complete the day is for Subby to put the boat on the mud or ram *Neptune's* side, so I think not.'

I leave them there and turn towards the bulkhead. A flicker of movement catches my eye as I glance towards the open-curtained wardroom. Pale-faced and hollow-eyed, Sub-Lieutenant Billings is sitting there. Our eyes meet for a second before he turns quickly away, and I know he has heard every word. 'Poor bastard!' I think to myself. 'He might be a wizard at navigation and a genius at mathematics, but no great shakes at anything else. In Studding's boat that adds up to failure.'

To everyone's credit the work goes ahead at a brisk pace. There are a few strange faces on board, mainly specialists delving into the innards of sick machinery. Most of our own men have a strange, white-chinned look about them now that they have shaved off a month's beard. Bedding is stretched out on the after casing, or hung over the jumping wire. A few privileged locals have come on board to unpick the stitching and tease out the innards of mattresses, before restuffing the canvas covers to freshen them up. *Audacity* smells a lot sweeter, and we have procured a new batch of films.

'Swain!'

'Yeah?'

'Jimmy wants you on the casing.'

'Okay.'

The sunshine dazzles me when I climb out of the hatch and look forward over the front of the bridge. The fore-casing is strewn with crates and bundles, and there is a chain-gang humping the stores down through the fore-hatch. Tyson is directing operations and I have to wait until he has a moment to spare for me.

'Your presence is required on *Neptune*, Grant. You are to report to a Lieutenant-Commander Hope on her quarterdeck. Don't take a wrong turning or we'll never see you again. Her innards are like a labyrinth, with passages and flats everywhere. Lord only knows how anyone ever finds his way about!'

I decide that so long as I keep climbing upwards I must eventually emerge onto her flightdeck. Once there it should be a simple matter of facing aft and keeping going until I find whatever passes for a quarterdeck in one of these floating airports.

After a bewildering series of wrong turnings I surface on to a gun-sponson where a twin bofors cocks its snouts into the sky. From here it is only a short climb up a ladder to the vast expanse of her flightdeck. If I expected to see an array of parked aircraft I am disappointed, but what I do see takes my breath away. It is like a huge football pitch. The massive bulk of the carrier over-shadows the dockside and I have to remind myself that this is only a light fleet carrier, and quite small compared to her larger Fleet sisters; not to mention the American monsters we are going to find when we reach the war-zone.

A youth in action working dress and an aircraft propeller emblazoned on his sleeve wanders by, so I ask him where I will find the quarterdeck.

He stares at me as though I am from outer space, then points a limp finger back to where I came from. 'You'll 'ave ter go back down there chief. You'll find a psssage be'ind that leads aft. That'll get you there.'

The cheeky young sod wears a cocky smile on his spotty face as he explains. He can't be more than eighteen and thinks it quite a joke to be asked by a chief PO with a row of medal ribbons on his chest where to find the most hallowed part of the ship. Quarterdecks are a throwback to the days when ships carried a crucifix, and the crew paid due reverence to that part of the ship. Now it is officer country, out of bounds to ratings unless they have a legitimate reason for being there. The deck is always a shade whiter, and the brasswork always that little bit brighter. Battleships and cruisers stretch awnings across the sacred area to provide a canopy for cocktail parties under fairy lights on balmy evenings when the gin flows freely. The officer of the watch paces the deck with a telescope tucked under his arms, accompanied by an entourage of quartermasters, bos'n's mates, side-boys and marine buglers. Even on shore bases a special area is marked off, and heaven help the rating who fails to salute or double across it.

The youngster watches me go down the ladder with an insolent sneer on his face, but I have neither the time nor the inclination to remonstrate with him.

The passage leads straight aft until I burst without warning onto the hallowed deck. *Neptune's* overhang provides the 'awning' in her case, but even here there is a wooden deck with neatly coiled ropage, while big apertures look out over the straits. The side-party look smart in their whites. They must be expecting VIPs, because they are wearing full number six dress. I am about to approach them when Calvin comes out of the shadows.

'You had better come down to my cabin,' he says tersely. It is an embarrassing moment for both of us as we carry out the formalities under the curious gaze of several other officers who are taking the air. He must have spent a lot of time in the sun on the way out for his face is deeply tanned. Right now he is anxious to get away from here, and so leads me quickly to a wide companionway that drops down into the muted sanctuary of the cabin-space, where the only sound comes from the hushed breathing of the air-conditioning. Eventually we arrive at his cabin door.

Inside there is the musty smell of bedding even though the scuttle stands open with a wind-scoop rigged to catch the breeze. Most of the space is taken up with a bunk, a small desk, washbasin, and a bench seat. He waves me onto the seat and carefully shuts the door behind him; standing with one hand on the bulkhead while he assembles his thoughts.

'I have received a disturbing letter from home, Ben,' he says keeping his stiff, unfriendly expression. 'There is concern for my father. He is more old and frail than he likes to admit and this business between you and Zoe is telling on his health. She seems to blame me for coming between you and spoiling the marriage arrangements. The whole family is worried; not least of all my mother, and the doctor says that dad cannot stand trauma.'

He sighs deeply. 'You and I both know that Zoe is not the type to moon about like a love-sick teenager, so I expect she is making no bones about the way she feels her big brother has done her wrong. The trouble with her is that she sees everything in black and white – a bit like my parents really. We would all like to see class barriers come down, but we have to live in a real world. My father cannot forget his humble beginnings, Ben. He tends to upset certain people, but he can get away with it most of the time, because everyone regards him as an eccentric. It is much harder for me, and not so cut and dried as Zoe would like to think.'

He looks at my blank face for a moment, then switches his eyes to the deck before going on more slowly, 'I know Mike Studding. He and I have been talking, and I have put him in the picture regarding Zoe and you. He tells me that despite your interview with Captain Kevel you have made no formal request to take the CW course.'

He waits for some sort of response, but when he realises that nothing is forthcoming continues, 'If your intentions are clear I will do all I can to help you. This stupid little war cannot go on for much longer, now that the Americans are building up their forces. The North Koreans are a second rate rabble who used the element of surprise to overwhelm an even more inferior rabble. Therefore *Audacity* may not reach the war-zone before it is all over. In any case, despite Mike's blind optimism, there is small scope for his submarine. So, if you take my advice, you will go for your commission. Complete the paperwork as soon as you can and get flown home to England.'

'Flown home!' That shakes me out of my shell. 'Who's going to pay for a chief to be flown home from the Far East?'

He is shuffling about, striving to overcome his distaste for what he has to do. 'Captain Kevel has been to see my father. They have been great friends for many years, and he has seen the effect this is having on the old man. I don't know if you realise that Kevel is Zoe's godfather, and loves her as much as we do. What he sees upsets him, and in the circumstances he has broken a golden rule and pulled strings. We, that is Mike Studding and I, know all about that special unit you are supposed to become part of.'

He looks directly into my eyes. 'Let us get one thing straight. No one is doing you any favours. You were selected for the team long before any of this came up. All we are doing is to pre-empt the issue for everyone's sake. It might not be ethical for Mike to approach you direct, so I offered to put you in the picture. You know as well as I that professionals and qualified specialists enter the service as officers. You have invaluable experience of submarine escape and many other things vital to the new set-up. In other words, Ben, you are being offered an immediate commission as soon as you make up your mind to take it.'

Strings! The bastard said it himself. They have been conniving behind my back for the sake of his old man and the family. Zoe would certainly have none of it, for she knows it is something I have condemned all my life. I have seen so many promoted for the wrong reasons, mostly to do with background or class, or making the right hand-signals. Unscrupulous toadies who climb the ladder on other men's backs. I detest them all, and the machinery that puts them where they are, and now I am being offered the doubtful privilege of joining their club.

I look at the smooth white bowl of the wash-basin, with its folded-back lid and varnished woodwork. Somehow it seems to represent all that lies between his world and mine. I have spent all my service life saluting, asking permission to speak, and carrying out all the subordinate requirements of my station, and up until now accepted it as part of the natural scheme of things. I had made up my mind to cross the barrier and enter his world; but under my conditions, and without any special favours. Doing it the way he suggest just sticks in my gullet.

'Well?' he asks when the silence becomes unbearable.

'I need time to think about it.'

'For God's sake, man! What is there to think about?' he roars. 'You have earned it through your own efforts. Mike tells me that it would make way for another man to gain a long overdue promotion, and it is what you have always wanted; a career in submarines, with the chance to contribute towards its future. What more could you ask?'

Solomon as coxswain! The idea puts a new obstacle in the way. The second coxswain has already shown that he cannot stand up to Welks. He is weak and unsure of himself, and that louse of an engineer will run rings round him. Tyson needs a strong man to rely on when the skipper drives the crew harder in his search for medals, and I am the only man on board who knows the way Welks operates. If I run out on them now I would feel like a deserter.

'I would need to think about,' I repeat doggedly.

He slumps back resignedly. 'Have it your own way. I think you are an inverted snob, Ben. People have bent over backwards for you, and you are throwing it back into their faces. You profess to love Zoe, yet you keep finding excuses. Could it be that your feelings for her are not as strong as you have led us to believe?'

I stand up. 'I don't think there is any point going on like this, Calvin. I am not being bloody-minded, and I appreciate your motives. I just have to get my thoughts in order, that's all.'

The door jumps back to its stoppers. 'Go on then,' he grunts. 'I'll not stick my neck out any more. I have already done far more than could reasonably be expected. No one can accuse me of prejudice now.' He eases his body outside and stands clear to let me go by.

Even under the overhang the sunlight is bright enough to make me blink when I emerge onto the quarterdeck and stride past curious eyes, to make my way forward to the ladder leading down to the jetty. The monster throbs with energy as I move through her body and out into the heat of the day. I pause for a moment to look down at *Audacity*. By British standards she is a big boat, but here, overwhelmed by the looming bulk of the carrier she looks minute.

In *Neptune* a man could serve a full commission and never visit parts of her, and still meet strangers. Whereas in *Audacity*, with her single passageway and simple layout; all confined within a sixteen foot diameter pressure-hull, and her two hundred and eighty foot length, there can be no secret parts. The mass of pipes and controls that decorate her innards are known to us by colour coding. We know the ones that feed HP and LP air to give her buoyancy and balance. Hydraulic oil to flex her muscles. Water to keep her and us from dehydrating. Fuel to power the diesels that drive her along and replenish her batteries. We know her to be a live thing with a pulsating heart, veins and arteries. The only thing she hasn't got is a brain. Without us she is a useless hulk, for we provide that brainpower and the nimble fingers that make her function. Every man is an important piece of her. In *Neptune* men become anonymous and she has a divided society. It showed in the young airman's insolent face when he thought he had put one over a dabtoe chief.

I stand for a moment, watching our men going about their tasks. Seamen passing stores from hand to hand along a chain leading down into her belly. Stokers standing by their pulsating fuel-line that snakes across the ballast tanks. They work with an air of quiet efficiency, and hardly a word needs to be spoken by their NCOs who are as dirty and sweaty as any of their men. In *Neptune* they would be taken to task for not standing back to supervise, while in *Audacity* you have to look at a man's arm badges to tell if he is a senior hand.

True, even in submarines there has to be a certain protocol, but nothing like the faceless variety that exists in the carriers. So long as I am allowed to remain in this 'club' I cannot use that as an excuse for refusing promotion. So maybe Calvin is right when he suggests that my motives are a mixture of inverted snobbery and lack of confidence, and if I had any guts I would leap at what is on offer, for my sake as well as Zoe's.

Inside the boat all is in chaos as a vast assortment of stores is stowed into every corner, and to add to the confusion the control-room is made impassable with deckboards raised and an array of oily bits of air-conditioner strewn all over the place. I retreat to the chiefs' mess, but hardly am I sat down before the navigator sticks his anxious face into the opening.

'Have you seen the signalman, Grant?'

I sigh, choking back a twinge of annoyance. 'No, sir. Not since he went to the Main Signals Distribution Office in barracks. I assume he would have had his meal there too.'

'That was hours ago. He should have been back now, and I cannot find him.'

The navigator is a nice bloke, but he has a complaining voice that grates on my nerves. I set my papers down carefully and make heavy work of easing myself out into the passageway. 'I'll sort it out, sir. Leave it to me.'

It takes me only a few minutes to check that he is nowhere in the vicinity of the boat, so I wend my way reluctantly into the barracks where every blade of grass seems to have been manicured, and white-painted flagposts and other parade-ground accoutrement gleams in the sunshine.

Unenthusiastic 'barrack-stanchions' respond to my queries with blank stares and an off-hand manner until eventually someone points vaguely towards the police-office, and the spot where the bus leaves at regular intervals for the city.

Inside a regulating petty officer sits at a desk with a wall of pigeon-holes and clip-boards at his back. He remembers Thorpe well, if only for his miserable face and surly manner. The signalman was wearing belt and gaiters to show he was on duty, and he carried a pass. That, and the cross flags on his arm-badge, were enough to allay any doubts the PO might have had. 'If he has jumped ship Chief, we can get him back for you,' he offers smugly.

I balk at that. Leading patrolmen are not noted for their

tact and diplomacy when dealing with wayward sailors, and Thorpe would become even more plenetic if I sent a posse of crushers chasing after him. It would also mean that we would have less room for manoeuvre, for once these vultures get involved it all becomes very official, and could be taken out of our hands entirely. I am scratching about for an answer, while the RPO waits impatiently with his hands hovering over the telephone, when I notice Tyson striding across the parade-ground towards the Admin' block.

I make an undignified dash and buttonhole him before he disappears through a doorway. He follows me to the picket-house, and we both argue with the naval police for several minutes as they try to convince us to allow them to 'take care of things.' We know what that means. These blokes seem to have a natural aversion to anyone in naval uniform, and adopt an attitude that assumes all matelots to be potential villains; out to plague authority.

We are in the middle of this argument, and getting nowhere, when the Master-at-Arms bursts into the fray; having been frantically summoned by messenger. He is a man of vast proportion, exceeded only by his own opinion of himself. Years of constant suspicion is instilled in him, and he is very conscious of his status. 'Jaunties' are the least popular members of big ships and barracks. They are lonely men, whose lives are governed by King's Regulations and Admiralty Instructions. However, Tyson is a match even for this pompous paragon, and he manages to persuade him to allow us four hours before calling out his bloodhounds.

'We had better go together,' suggests Tyson, and we get a few old-fashioned looks when he climbs into the bus with me. Officers do not travel with the 'troops,' but he is in mood to stand on ceremony today.

We rumble along a dusty road and through small Malay villages where handsome men and beautiful women with olive skin and oriental eyes potter about, while laughing children scamper from hut to hut as though they belong to everyone. There is an air of indolence and contentment that sets them apart from their more industrious neighbours, the Chinese and Indians. Simple people who live by age-old custom that excludes authority. When they have a problem they go next door to solve it, and everyone gets involved until something is sorted out. Because they are so easy-going they have become the minority in their own country, and have little say in the running of things. Theirs is the same insular apathy that I have noticed in other island communities that has allowed more sophisticated outsiders to take over.

The bus drops us at the Britannia Club, and having got this far we are at a bit of a loss to know what to do next. It seems pointless to wander off into the teeming cauldron of humanity that chokes the streets on the off-chance of finding Thorpe. Everyone seems to be trying to outdo each other in creating the most bustle and noise, and the overpowering roar of traffic drums in our ears. Trishaws, taxis, buses, and a raucous mixture of other transport battle between rich profusions of gawdy signs, and no one seems to have time to stand still for one second.

'I'll go into the canteen if you like, sir.' I offer. 'Someone might have noticed him.'

It is a vague hope, and we are clutching at straws, but he nods and crosses the monsoon ditch with me. Standing with his back to the wall while I disappear inside.

The place is cool and dark: As near to a NAAFI as makes no difference, and there are several servicemen sitting at tables, leaning over the bar with 'Tiger Ale' in front of them. I saunter through the place searching the shadows. The walls cut out the sound and it is quiet and peaceful in here. Today my luck is in, for I find Thorpe sitting on his own in one corner, wrapped up in his own misery. He doesn't blink an eye when he notices me approaching, and seems utterly resigned to whatever comes his way. The booze has done nothing to improve his disposition, and it looks as though the other occupants are going out of their way to avoid him.

'Come on, Bunts,' I say quietly. 'Tyson's outside, and you're in enough trouble already. Don't balls things completely.'

His sad eyes stare into the distance, lifeless in their dark sockets. There is something deeply tragic in the way this veteran sits alone, clutching a half-filled glass of beer as though it offers a lifeline. When I reach under his armpit to help him to his feet he rises automatically and follows me out into the bedlam where Tyson takes one look and hails a passing taxi.

It is left to Thorpe to break the silence after several minutes on the road across the island. 'I had to be alone for a while,' he says, as though that's all the excuse he needs. 'I want to have it all out now. It ain't fair to make me wait until we get to Hong Kong to find out what's gonna happen to me. I want to clear my yard-arm, and it's gonna be bloody awful livin' with mates who think you are a mess-deck thief.'

'There's no time for that now,' insists Tyson harshly. 'It will have to wait. It might not be such a bad thing if you think about it. If, as you say, you are innocent, it will allow time for other factors to come to light. Time is on your side, and you are facing a serious charge. This kind of behaviour is hardly likely to enhance your chances when you argue your case. When the time comes you will have an officer to represent you, and I will give you every assistance I can, providing you don't try a stunt like this again. We are on a war-footing now, and you could be charged with desertion for what you've done. As it is we are going to have to argue with the Provost Martial to get you off if we are not careful.'

The signalman leans back into the upholstery and stays mute for the remainder of the journey. The Master-at-Arms grunts and mutters a bit when we explain that there has been a mistake; and Thorpe misread his orders, thinking he had to go to the main post-office. He huffs and puffs a bit, but it's a hot day, and in the end he is too lazy to insist on dragging it out; especially when Tyson stresses that the boat is on its way to Korea.

Once back on board Thorpe slips back into his cocoon. I clamp down and tell him that he is under open arrest. He is to report to me every hour, and a telegraphist takes over the job of collecting signals from the SDO.

Through sheer hard work the boat is made ready for sea by twenty hundred hours and Studding obtains permission to sail immediately. We slip quietly away from the temptations of shore with our radar painting the outsized blips of the reflectors on the marker-buoys that lead us down channel and out into the south China Sea.

We head north, with Borneo to starboard and Malay to port, towards the sea-lanes between the Philippines and Indo-China. There is the makings of a storm brewing as we lurch and roll to a white capped ocean, but the wind is warm to the cheek and has a growing whine in its voice as it blusters through the periscope standards. To me it is an ominous sound as we leave behind the tropical extravagance of Singapore and push on towards the bleak, saturnine cliffs of China.

V

There are almost fifteen hundred miles to go. Four days to bottle our energies and set aside differences. The atmosphere inside the boat ferments as we move away from the land with its sultry heat and lingering smells. Watch follows watch with mind-numbing repetition. Change-over reports are carried out in toneless voices, without even the customary gripe when someone turns up a few minutes late for his lookout. The sea builds to a full gale that comes sweeping in from the east to drench the bridge-party and send them below at the end of each stint soaked through and steaming in the warmth of the hull. No one cares anymore. The only thing uppermost in everyone's mind is that every hour brings us closer to that vital run ashore.

On the morning of the fifth day I rise early from my bunk to ask permission to go up top where I find the scene shrouded in a veil of driving rain. We are out of reach of the wind now, but it is still there, blowing the drizzle like smoke from the towering ramparts of rocky cliffs as they close in on all sides while we plough through a bleak expanse of grey sea.

A hundred yards to port, running along on the same course, and looking like an ancient pirate ship as she takes shape in the mist, is a big junk. She looks ghostlike with her battened lugsail swinging to the wind as she shoulders her way in towards the land, curtseying to the sea like an elderly lady. I can see people standing beneath her poop, their pale faces turned away from us as they crouch into their black, loose-fitting smocks and trousers; hunched against the stinging rain. I watch her lift and drop with no effort at all, breasting the sea as though she is part of it, while *Audacity's* bows scoop water and send it deluging aft to half-drown the lookouts.

I drink it all in as I savour big lungfuls of clean air. The forbidding heights of headland and island lift themselves out of the ocean as we go by, and I can sense the vastness of the huge continent that lies beyond. This has to be the only way to enter Hong Kong. To watch it grow out of the mist like a land of ghosts with smoke spilling from the rim of the hills as they close in on either side. It would surely be wrong to drop out of the sky into the animated congestion that lies beyond, and miss this magnificent overture of scraggy cliffs to set the scene. Junks are becoming more prolific now as we steer into the roads. This is no willow-pattern fairyland china, but a huge portentous monster that throws out a challenge as we make our landfall.

'Coxswain!'

'Shit!' I curse beneath my breath as I hear Subby's public school voice. 'Sir?'

'Tremendous, isn't it?'

I shrug aside my annoyance and sidle round to the front of the bridge to where he is standing his watch with oilskins flapping and an outsized sou'wester pulled well down over his head, making him look like a skinny moose. A lookout moves aside to let me in and allow us to talk.

'Have you been here before, Grant?'

'Yes, sir. But not since it changed ownership.'

'Of course – I'd forgotten for the moment.'

I can't make up my mind about him. He comes from genteel stock, and even Dartmouth has not succeeded in roughening the edges. Welks has a lot of fun at his expense, and the other officers tend to ignore him for much of the time, for he has limited conversation, and he is painfully self-conscious. In his locker he has a collection of pressed flowers and plants which he gathers whenever he gets ashore, and he doesn't seem to understand that other people cannot share his rapture when he returns with a new specimen.

Right now though, we have something in common. We are both enthralled by what we are looking at; unlike the majority of our ship-mates, who prefer to remain below until the very last moment, rather than face the driving rain. They seem impervious to the wonder of far-off lands that most of us only know from pictures in books and films.

'What do you think it will be like?' he asks suddenly, after we have spent a few moments absorbing the scene together.

'What, sir?'

'The war. You've experienced it. What's it like?'

'Jesus!' The oath slips out before I have time to think. I look away for a second. 'There's no way anyone can describe a bloody war, sir. Ninety per cent boredom and ten per cent blind terror is what most people say. This ain't the same. The Hitler one got inside you no matter where you were. It affected everyone from cradle to grave; you just couldn't get away from it. On the other hand, this is an isolated war. As new to me as it is to you.'

'Why are we becoming involved do you think?' His face swings towards me and a cataract of cold water spills over me. I dodge back quickly and he jerks off his sou'wester apologetically. Drizzle is running down over his pale skin into his collar. He looks no more than a kid as he looks at me with anxious eyes.

'They tell us it is to stop the spread of communism, sir.'

'Do you believe that?'

'I'm not paid to think, sir.'

'Come on, Coxswain,' he protests. 'I am reliably informed that you are about to take the cloth and become one of us. You will have to voice opinions then.'

'No, sir. Opinions are for admirals and politicians.'

He goes quiet and replaces the sou'wester onto his streaming hair as he stares out across the bow. The lookouts have given up making formal reports now, for we are surrounded by dozens of small craft, and they confine themselves to anything that looks as though it might cause a problem. It is getting too uncomfortable even for me. He must call down for the captain soon, and I am about to move away when he adds in an anxious, desperate voice, 'You don't think anything can go wrong, do you? Nothing to stop the men from getting their run ashore?'

I look back at him. 'I bloody well hope not, sir.'

His voice is soft. 'I hope so too. I – I was just wondering if a court martial would hold us up.'

'I don't think anything will stop the captain from getting us to the war, sir. Courts martial can wait.' I lean towards him. 'I'd call the captain if I were you, sir. The traffic is getting thick.'

Suddenly his hand is gripping my sleeve tightly to hold me back. I try to shake it off angrily. The lookouts are darting curious looks at this unwonted show of familiarity. I can feel his hand shaking as he hangs on grimly. 'The men have to have their liberty, Grant. You must do all you can to see nothing else goes wrong.'

I take hold of his arm and wrench it away, just as Studding climbs out of the hatch. Subby wheels to face forward, and I squeeze past the captain to go below.

There is a lot of movement inside the boat as preparations go on for entering harbour. I am still smarting from the seemingly pointless conversation as I take my place at the wheel. It was a stupid immature outburst, one of Subby's specials, yet it nags me as I wait for the first orders to come down the voice-pipe. 'Surely nothing will prevent the men getting ashore now?'

We berth alongside the wall somewhere between the Kowloon Ferry landing and the China Fleet Club, in a small basin with a high barrier of buildings between us and the street that runs parallel to the shore. A continuous rumble of traffic throbs day and night amidst the pulsating murmur of an invisible multitude going about its affairs. Big, gaudy ferries criss-cross the bustling harbour where the lean shapes of two frigates rest at their moorings; one of ours, and an American. The waterway is almost as congested as the streets, with thousands of sam-pans dodging between bigger traffic, and through it all a procession of slow-moving junks glide by on timeless journeys. A big merchantman with a forest of masts and samson-posts, and a square white bridge ploughs in towards the commercial docks, a limp Red-Duster drooping from her stern.

Inshore the tail buildings lift towards soaring hills; so tall, they keep the stars at bay when night falls. Up on those heights opulent villas nestle, with patios and balconies overlooking the harbour. While, in contrast, shanty towns crowd in concentrated squalor, where people struggle to eke out an existence by a mixture of legal and not so legal enterprise. Some of our men will indulge themselves in those ramshackle tin hunts and return with more than they bargained for. A regular parade of prostitutes takes place down by the docks, with taxis standing by to ferry clients up into the hills. A sort of human market-place, as traditional as Petticoat Lane.

A man can wallow in debauchery or drink himself stupid. He can soar to the Peak in a cable-car to stare down in wonder at the swarming panorama. Here time and space are at a premium. No one has a second to spare or a secluded place to relax, except the rich. Like me the crew come up to stare at it, eager to get ashore.

They have more than a month's pay in their pockets and money-belts. It is burning a hole, and the first lot scramble ashore like locusts when they are released. First stop is the China Fleet Club, to wallow in hot baths and regain some composure before launching into the simmering cauldron that awaits them. Rickshawmen are ready-made guides who know every remote corner to satisfy the most demanding appetite. Nothing shocks or surprises them, for they are immune from the worst excesses of ship-bound sailors with money to spend, and weeks of enforced inactivity to work out of their systems.

Within two hours the first casualties begin to crawl back over the gangway in soiled whites and with bloodstained faces. One sorry specimen shows me half a tattoo on his buttock and no idea where to go to have it completed. I suppose we should count ourselves lucky that no one actually gets killed, and the following morning I find two distinct groups when I take stock. Grey-featured survivors with hangovers, who need to be watched, or they take crafty whiffs of recuperating oxygen from the DSEA sets, while their mates in the port watch look on with 'holier-than-thou' expressions and wait their turn to sample the dubious delights of Hong Kong.

We employ two 'sampan girls' to get rid of our 'gash' and paint over any bald patches they find on the hull. Each evening they squat on the casing, unwind their pigtails, scrub themselves clean and comb their long, jet-black hair down over their shoulders until it shines like ebony. I wince when I see them get to work on the soles of their feet with our regulation deck scrubbers.

The mail comes on board at noon, and there is a letter for me. It begins 'Darling Ben,' and ends with an 'I love you;' but in between it is a bitter admonishment for the way I am dithering about. Neither she nor her parents give a damn whether I become an officer or not, but they do think that it is about time I stopped using it as an excuse and began to think of others. They want to plan for the future, and she thinks it is about time she had a firm commitment so that she and her folk can give straightforward replies to bewildered relatives and friends. All it does is make me more confused than ever.

By mid-afternoon these things are pushed into the background by a new development. The specialists working on the water distiller and air conditions have found evidence of sabotage. A duplex feed strainer has been tampered with, and the chemical injection tank contaminated with abrasives, amongst other obvious deliberate damage. Whoever is responsible must have had a fair idea of the mechanics involved, and was able to gain access without rousing suspicion. Whoever it was made little effort to disguise his work, so that it looks almost as if he wanted to be found out.

The artificers had been reluctant at first to put it down to more than just coincidence when things began to go wrong, but when the unbiased experts arrived to strip down the units they had no such reservations. When their report is examined by the skipper and Tyson it becomes only too clear that someone is attempting to delay our progress to the war. It is not the first time this sort of thing has happened. Men have tried to stop ships sailing before, for all kinds of reasons, but Studding takes it as a personal attack.

As though that were not enough, Tyson calls me to the wardroom when two small parcels turn up on the table. One is a soft leather wallet containing Egyptian pound notes and some sterling, and the other is also a wad of notes held together with an elastic band.

'I left my cap upturned on the table for just two minutes while I went to the heads, and when I returned those parcels were inside,' he proclaims. 'Ask those two men who had money stolen to come here.'

Both men identify their property and agree that neither package has been disturbed in any way.

'Well?' demands Tyson when the two happy men have gone.

'Damned if I know, sir. I can find no rhyme nor reason for it.' I tell him. 'But there is one thing that stands out clearly. Whoever it is wants to be found out, and he hasn't the guts to come forward on his own. It looks to me like a plea for help: I've seen this sort of thing before.'

'Yes, and there's another thing too,' he says quietly. 'This lets Thorpe off the hook. He's been up top all the time, and there are plenty of witnesses to verify that.' He shakes his head. 'I think we ought to tell the captain at once, before he finds out for himself.'

We find him on the jetty, deep in conversation with two officers from the base. We wait patiently until he gets rid of them, and he listens without comment while Tyson explains. Afterwards his face takes on a strange look, growing harder as he stares into space. The expression in his eyes makes me cringe. He walks away from us to stare down into the murky water of the basin with his forehead creased into a deep frown, then, as though he has suddenly made up his mind, he swings about and strides deliberately up to Tyson.

'No one go ashore until the culprit has been found. I will hold an enquiry in the fore-ends in half an hour, and we had better find some answers. You, Coxswain, will accompany me, and so will Mr Welks. We will interview every member of the crew until we find the man who has perpetrated this act of treason. In the meantime, Number One, you and the navigator will conduct a thorough inspection of the boat. There may be other signs of sabotage, or even a clue that could help the investigation. I am assuming that all these acts have been the work of one individual, so you can tell the men that unless he comes forward of his own free will there will be no shoreleave.'

'With due respect, sir. Surely it is not necessary to keep everyone on board? You said yourself that the culprit has to be a specialist. I suggest that we allow them to go about their duties normally, allow the port watch their shore-leave, and concentrate on the senior hands.'

'No,' snaps Studding. 'That won't do at all. I do not believe for one minute that anyone can remain completely isolated in this boat. Someone somewhere, apart from the criminal himself, knows about it, and nothing puts more pressure on a sailor than to have his shore-leave stopped. If this man has any remaining decency he will not stand to have his mates punished for what he has done.'

Now it is my turn to stick out my neck. 'But, sir, half the crew have already been ashore: it wouldn't be right!'

He rounds on me. 'Don't dictate to me what's right and

wrong, Coxswain!' he roars in a voice that has heads turning all over the dockside. 'This has brought things to a head. It has been one damn thing after another since we left Port Said. I suppose that furore in the fore-ends was innocent. No! There has been a deliberate attempt to keep us from Korea. Has it occurred to either of you that there might be a political motive behind this?'

Tyson and I exchange looks. 'I – I don't quite understand, sir,' states the first lieutenant in a subdued voice.

'Good God, do I have to spell it out?' Studding turns to face us. 'We are fighting communism. There was an attempt to sabotage *Neptune* before she sailed from Portsmouth. Do you think we are immune?' He looks from me to Tyson as though he cannot believe we have not thought along these lines. 'It seems quite logical to me that we could have someone in *Audacity* with every reason to put her out of the fight. That is why we must root out this cancer before we sail.'

He strides away, leaving us staring after him, open-mouthed. When we recover I say quietly to Tyson. 'If it was a political thing, sir, it wasn't much of an effort, was it? Seems to me that anyone with those sort of ideals could have achieved more than just delaying tactics.'

He decides to ignore me. 'Will you tell the men about their cancelled leave, or shall I?'

'Perhaps it would come better from me, sir. I'll go round the boat and tell each man personally rather than let them hear it over the tannoy.'

'Very well.'

It is one experience I never wish to repeat. They do not need to be told of the events leading up to Studding's decision. Everyone is just as anxious as he to find out whose wrecking their boat. What they cannot understand is why their captain is depriving them of their well-earned leave when it is quite obvious to anyone that the majority of them must be innocent. They listen with a mixture of outrage and disappointment. Not only for what they are being denied, but because the man they once respected is treating them so badly.

Many of *Audacity's* men are long-serving, and have devoted their energies into making her a top boat in the Fleet for no other reasons then professional pride and a high regard for their captain. I have a nasty taste in my mouth as I go from one group to the next, for they look as if they have been physically struck by the man who demanded, and got, total commitment from them. No captain can achieve anything on his own, and it took more than just blind obedience to give him an edge over other commanders, and now they feel he has played them false, taken his spite out on them by punishing the innocent for no more reason than that he feels affronted. Today he has lost much of what remained of their respect and loyalty, and can no longer rely on them to perform his miracles. Some of the heart goes out of *Audacity* just at the time when she needs it most.

I had arranged to go ashore with Hancock for a look at the place. We had decided to skip the usual haunts and take a ride from terminus to terminus on the top deck of a tram, so that we could look down at the bustling activity on the crowded pavements. Everything spills out onto the kerb in the animated canyons between the tall buildings, and everyone has something to sell. Afterwards we were to take the Kowloon ferry for a meal in one of the thousands of restaurants where we could look out across the harbour to where a scattering of twinkling lights climb up until they merge with the stars.

Instead we meet in sombre mood and Hancock's face is dour and worried. His torpedomen are embittered, and make snide comments when he goes amongst them to try to make light of the situation. We tell ourselves that the culprits must be found quickly in a boat where a man cannot sneeze without half the crew hearing him, but it offers small compensation, for we have a nasty feeling that liberty is going to be bought with the impeachment of a shipmate who is in need of compassion rather than punishment.

When I go through the boat I study the men's faces and find nothing in their expressions other than rancour and indignation. Going by looks Thorpe is the most likely suspect, for he is on the defensive, and goes about the boat with a sullen face and saying nothing, even though he is the one man who has been cleared. His resentment goes deeper than just the feeling of outrage that the others have. I try to bring him out of it, and his mates go out of their way to redress the balance, but it makes no difference. It is enough that they could suspect him at all. For a man with his background there is nothing more foul than a messdeck thief, and that label sticks once it has been attached, no matter how many times he is proved innocent.

There is a new game being played in the boat now. Senior hands have to issue sharp reminders when over-loud comments are voiced, which are designed to reach the wardroom and Studding. I have not heard the captain's nickname, 'Starchy,' used for some time, but now it takes on a new connotation when they spit it out, and his prestige sinks to an all-time low.

The starboard watch keep very quiet about their run ashore so as not to offend their less fortunate shipmates, and the rift between the engine-room and deck brigade grows until they will not work together, an unheard of situation in submarines, where duties overlap so much. Everyone knows that the saboteur is most likely a technician, and there is an unfounded suspicion that the 'black-gang' is closing ranks to protect one of their own kind. In their frustration the men are looking for easy targets, and it gets so bad I go to Tyson with my worries.

'If things go on as they are we are going to have a riot that will make that fore-ends debacle look like a vicar's tea-party, sir.'

'All right, Grant,' he says after a moment's thought. 'I will speak to them. Perhaps I can take some of the steam out of the situation.'

The hubbub dies at the first chuckle of the tannoy. 'As you know we have a saboteur loose in the boat who must be stopped before he does something to endanger *Audacity* and her crew,' his steady voice tells them. 'It is inevitable that he will be caught eventually, therefore, I am offering him the opportunity to come forward of his own volition. I promise he will receive a fair hearing, and in order to make it easier, I will make myself available in one of the dockside offices, the one with the wire mesh over the window. There is a frequent coming and going of personnel so it should not be difficult for him to report without drawing attention to himself, and the offer is open to anyone who has something to tell me. I firmly believe that this man needs help, so if anyone has any information at all, you are not doing him, nor yourselves, any favours by sitting on it.'

Reluctantly Studding agrees to postpone the enquiry for another hour to give Tyson's offer a chance, but after half that time it is obvious that no one is coming forward. The fore-ends are cleared of all personnel other than those taking part, and we set up a table and stools and call in the first man. Two of the artificers sit in the background to render assistance with the technical details, and because there is little point in carrying out his search. Tyson joins us.

We begin with the engine-room branch for obvious reasons, and their attitudes range from outright belligerence to floundering anxiety. One by one they answer Studding's probing questions, and at times one of the artificers comes in with a technical point, but Welks makes no attempt to contribute at all. He adopts a stony, indignant attitude, as though he is piqued at having his men singled out for interrogation like this. Some falter and look as guilty as hell, while others forcefully proclaim their innocence, and by the time we have gone through the engine-room and started on the seamen we know we are flogging a dead horse.

It is becoming a repetitive farce by the time we get to one of the torpedomen who seems more numbed than the rest, and takes an age to answer the simplest questions. In the middle of one extended silence Studding rises to his feet and slams a fist onto the table. 'Damn it, man, what are you all trying to hide from me?'

The torpedoman jumps six inches out of his seat and holds his arms across his face as if he expects to be hit, and for a moment the captain fumes over him in a towering rage, before he regains control and yells, 'Get him out of here. There is something going on in this boat, and I'll find out what if I have to punish the whole crew.'

He moves to the foot of the ladder leading up through the fore-hatch, turns and points a threatening finger at us. 'It is up to you now. *Audacity* is going to war, and no bloody Marxist is going to stop me! If I hear one dissenting voice, or see anyone carrying out his duty with less than total commitment I will assume that he is in on the conspiracy. It will go particularly hard on senior men, so be warned!'

We watch his feet clatter out of sight. The torpedoman is wide-eyed and stunned, needing to be told twice by Tyson to shove off and leave us with our thoughts.

'We are missing something somewhere,' declares Tyson. 'Something that should be staring us in the face. Let's go through our notes and try a process of elimination. We could begin by putting aside the depositions of seamen and communication ratings.'

'Oh no we couldn't!' interjects Welks, and I have to wipe some of his spittle from my face. 'That's what you would like, wouldn't you? To lay the blame on my lads. Well I'm not convinced. The damage could have been done by anyone with average intelligence, even a bloody dabtoe!'

'Everyone's under suspicion, Chief. It is just that we are

trying to bring it down to the most likely ones. We have to begin somewhere for heaven's sake! Somewhere in this boat there is a man trying to live with his guilt amongst his shipmates. I don't believe anyone can sustain that for long; the strain must be unbearable. If we keep up the pressure he is bound to crack, so let's start with this and forget misguided loyalties for the moment.'

The bulkhead door swings open to admit Hancock. 'We've got a problem aft, sir. In the controlroom.'

'Now what, for God's sake!'

'Several blokes are dressed in their number sixes, all sayin' they're going ashore. I tried to intervene, but everyone just stood in my way. It looks as though they have bin holdin' a meetin' while you were holdin' your enquiry. You can't go that way, sir,' he adds when Tyson makes a dash for the door. 'They have blocked the passageway.'

I am already half-way up the ladder before he stops talking, launching myself out of the hatch in time to see several men clambering down from the bridge. I reach the gangway before the first man gets there. It is Solomon, dressed smartly in full whites – no mean feat in the oily confines of the hull. It must be a gesture, for most men prefer to go ashore in half-whites – white fronts and blue trousers.

'Don't try to stop us, Swain,' he warns.

'You're behaving like idiots,' I snap.

'That's our problem.'

By now there is a bunch of men gathered at the gangway. Their faces tell me that I stand no chance of stopping them, but I make one more effort. 'This is not the way to go about it, Solomon. You are on top line for promotion, and you'll lose all that.' I look round at the others. 'You all stand a good chance of going to chokey if you're not careful: Think about it!'

'We are all in this together!' shouts one brave soul from the back of the crowd. I can see men from the starboard watch hovering about on the fringe, standing ready to back up their mates. Completely at a loss I turn to Tyson, expecting to see him explode. Instead I am amazed to find him nodding slowly, with a wry smile on his lips.

'Coxswain!' he says in a voice that carries to everyone. 'Shore-leave is granted to the port watch from sixteen hundred hours until oh seven three oh. Dress of the day – number ones, negative tops.'

A seven beller! For a moment they gape back in disbelief, then, with one accord a mighty cheer erupts, and they make a rush towards the gangway.

Solomon stands firm; blocking the way. 'Pack that up!' he blares, and the cheers dies. 'You idiots! Can't you see we've won nothing?' He turns to Tyson. 'We don't want you to stick your neck out for us, sir.'

'Don't kid yourself!' sneers Tyson. 'It is the lesser of two evils. I am not going to tolerate a full-scale walk-out that will damage the reputation of *Audacity* and her captain. You may feel hard done by, but, remember, somewhere in the boat is a man determined to stop us from reaching Korea. So far he has done nothing to endanger anyone, but who can say how far he will go. If we don't find him your lives could be on the line.'

They shuffle their feet disconsolately; avoiding each other's eyes and waiting for someone to make a move. Inevitably it is Solomon who steps forward. 'The men mean no harm, sir.' He turns to the others. 'What do you say, lads? Do we give it a miss this time?'

'Stow that!' roars Tyson in a voice that reverberates from the buildings. 'You are not a bloody trade union. I have given leave to the port watch, and it stands. It is entirely up to you whether you go ashore or not?'

He switches his stare to Solomon. 'We will have no demonstrations in this boat. Behave yourself while on shore, and come back on time. You have neither won nor lost anything, but try anything like this again and I'll throw the book at you. Remember: only one thing really matters in all this – the boat!'

It is a subdued procession that staggers across the plank and spreads out into a straggling group of unsmiling, guilt-ridden men. I watch them go sadly, and their starboard watch mates slope away to their duties in morbid silence.

'Come on, Grant. I haven't the stomach to face the captain on my own. If I had any guts I would stick my neck out and take what's coming to me like all the good books say, but I am sick of useless gestures, and there is something very basic to be sorted out here.'

Our opportunity doesn't come until well into the first dog-watch when Studding comes storming across the gangway after running into a band of *Audacity's* sailors on shore. It takes a combined effort to quell a tirade of threats and promises of retribution, but eventually he has to stop for breath, and before he can get going again we leap in.

'It was either allow them leave or face a full-scale mutiny, sir,' explains Tyson during the lull. 'So far we have kept our domestic problems to ourselves, and managed to avoid involving the shore authorities. The artificers have agreed to sit on their findings for a while, and allow us time to find the man responsible. If we allow things to get out of our control, all you have worked for could be destroyed. We will never see Korea, because we will be bogged down in red tape and a full-scale enquiry. As it is, we have toned the whole thing down, and kept it internal. It is a tenuous situation but at least it is under control.'

Studding slumps. His face is grey and he looks shattered. 'We are finished, Andy. There is no way to keep this from the authorities now. I will have to make a complete report, and this time I must not gloss over the facts. I feared this would happen; that is why I was so determined to find the saboteur. With him out of the way we may have stood a chance – but now –' His voice tails off as he stares into space.

Eventually he look at our faces with a rueful grin. 'Don't

concern yourselves on my account. I can see now that you did all there was to do in the circumstances: The alternatives are too awful to contemplate. We do not always think straight when we are up against it, and it is easy to think only of oneself.'

Tyson looks at the disillusioned figure of his captain for a moment. 'Why don't you sleep on it, sir? You can do nothing before morning anyway. By then things might have sorted themselves out.'

Studding lifts his head to look out at *Neptune*. We had hardly noticed her arrival earlier in the day. 'I am invited to dine in the carrier tonight. I watched her come in with her Marine band playing, and her saluting guns firing while we were sorting out our sordid little problems. She looked smart and warlike, while we were skulking with our tails between our legs because we have a rotten apple in our company. I have never felt such shame, Andy.' He suddenly snaps his head round. 'Get into your glad-rags, Number One. You deserve to share my humiliation.'

I feel I'm in the way now. 'Excuse me, sir. I'd like to go below.'

'Embarrassing you, am I, Coxswain?' he says smoothly. 'Off you go then. You'll not find it so easy to slide out from under if you take your commission.'

I drop my eyes and turn away to go below, where I find Hancock pacing the fore-ends. He comes towards me as though he has been waiting. 'You look as though you could do with a run ashore, Ben. What's to stop us now?'

'I'm in no bloody mood for sight-seeing.'

'The kind of sights I have in mind should improve your outlook for a while. Come on, mate – indulge yourself.'

'All right,' I grunt, suddenly sick of the whole thing. 'Give me five minutes to get my togs on.'

We visit strange places and drink some cheap hootch, and by the time we wend our weary way back to the boat I am too befuddled and tired to care about anything. Hong Kong throbs with life, and I know we haven't even scratched the surface, but we have both had more than enough. It has not lifted my depression, but it has dulled my senses, and I feel satisfactorily numbed.

Inside the gates the basin slumbers in isolated quietness and the boat looks sad as she rests against the wall, with the trot sentry standing guard over her.

'There's a light in that hut,' muses Hancock in a thick voice.

I focus my weary eyes in the direction he points and see a pale yellow glow filtering from the windows with the wire-mesh covering. 'So!' I grunt. 'Someone has left a light on – so what?'

'Yeah,' he agrees, swaying. 'Still, I think I'll go over and take a look. Some boozy bastard might be sleeping it off inside.'

I shrug indifferently, but follow behind him as he wanders across. The door stands slightly ajar, with a shaft of weak light spreading across towards the harbour. He pushed it wide with a hefty kick and we both sober up at once. Subby's polished shoes dangle eight inches from the deck, and his eyes are bulging out of their sockets as he twists slowly round with his tongue hanging out of his bloated, purple face. A thin wire noose bites into his scrawny neck.

'Jesus Christ!' yells Hancock as we both elbow our way inside. I grab Subby's feet to hoist up his weight to slacken the wire so that Hancock can jump onto the desk and get at it.'

'It's eaten right into his bloody neck!' he pants, struggling with the noose. 'I can't get the soddin' thing loose, and it's buried into the wooden beam above too.'

He drops down onto the deck. 'Bet you ain't got your pusser's dirk. I might have twisted it off with a marlin spike.'

I shake my head. 'Let's scratch about, there might be something amongst all this rubbish we can use.'

'You gonna let him go?'

I nod. 'He's as dead as he'll ever be.' I lower the body cautiously. I have a horrible feeling the wire hasn't got far to go before it decapitates the poor bastard. There must be enough gristle to take the weight, however, and I leave him dangling while I search the shadows until I find a rusting tool-box with some equally rusting tools inside. They are corroding into a solid mass, but I manage to extricate a bent-shanked screwdriver with a split handle. Utterly useless for the purpose it was designed for it suits our needs to perfection. I scramble onto the table and insert the shaft between the wire and the beam. One quick twist and Subby slumps to the deck with a sickly thud. I jump down again to help Hancock stretch the body out into a tidy shape. There isn't much we can do to improve his looks, so we cover his face with a piece of grubby towelling that hangs in grimy dejection at the side of a cracked wash-basin. That done we both straighten up and contemplate the corpse.

'We had better not disturb anything else,' says Hancock rather belatedly. 'It's a police job now.'

'Hang on a mo,' I say quickly. 'There might be a note or something in his pockets.'

'You'll be in trouble if you mess about too much, Ben,' he warns as I rummage through Subby's clothing.

'I'm giving him artificial respiration.' I can feel the soft, pasty flesh, clammy through the thin lining, and there is a faint smell of stale sweat exuding from the corpse. He will stiffen up soon I expect, but right now he feels like a lump of putty.

'Sorry, Subby,' I mutter. 'You were never much to look at when you were alive, but you're a repulsive looking bastard now.'

'Leave him alone!'

I freeze, then swing round to find Tyson and the skipper framed in the doorway, still wearing their monkey suits and black ties.

'What the hell do you think you are doing, Grant?' demands Tyson in a voice loaded with minacity.

Studding is pushing through to take a closer look. When he shifts his gaze to me there is a grim expression on his face. I straighten up and stare back at him. 'I am looking for a suicide note, sir,' I explain lamely. 'I thought it might be best if we found one before the police arrive.'

His face relaxes. 'Don't bother. It was waiting in my cabin when I returned, but for all that it tells us he need not have bothered.' He holds a small sheet of notepaper to me. 'Maybe you can shed some light on it.'

'Try and ignore me now,' is all it reads in capital letters, with a scrawled signature below.

'He was never the garrulous type,' remarks Tyson drily. Even in death Subby doesn't inspire much respect from his messmates.

'You had better telephone the police, Grant,' sighs Studding. 'We will have half the Hong Kong constabulary swarming all over the boat now. If that silly young idiot had problems, why the hell didn't he try to talk them out with someone?'

My mind snaps back to the conversation I had with Subby on the bridge as I run for the phone. Like everyone else I made little effort to listen to what he had to say. There's a tight feeling in my throat when I think of what a lonely man he was. Awkward and shy amongst a crowd of extroverts whose bawdy talk always embarrassed him, despite his public school background and Dartmouth. Whatever he was cut out for, it certainly wasn't the navy – let alone submarines. He would have looked more at home amongst dusty relics in some historical archive. His detailed notes and records would have been faultlessly accurate, but his conversation as dry as the dust of old bones.

When the police arrive they are a mixture of civilian and our provost authorities. As predicted, they swarm all over the place, so that it is impossible to assume any sort of normal routine. The men eye these intruders with open suspicion, and talk amongst themselves about Subby's suicide. They resent the questioning and close ranks in the manner of all sailors when shore authorities invade their domain. There are angry scenes when we stop the police from entering sections that contain highly secret equipment, and that is where our own police take over, much to the indignation of a pompous inspector who puts himself about like a bloody admiral.

'Toffee-nosed sod!' snorts Hancock. 'Half of them would be walking the beat at home. Out here any half-baked bloke winds up with house servants and a life-style way above his rank. I met a bloke on shore who was a dockyard foreman in Plymouth. He's a bloody manager out here. They inherited a house-boy who was about seventy years old. The previous family had treated him like shit, and when they offered to take him on again he refused. He told them he had got what he set out for. He had put up with the abuse and ill-manners, saved all his pennies, and sent his two sons through college and law school in the UK. Both of them had been called to the bar. No, Ben. There's a lot of jumped-up second-rate sods living like kings out here, earning their countrymen a reputation for being arrogant ignoramuses who should not be allowed to mix with decent people.'

A blue van takes Subby's body away, and there is a general reluctance for anyone to go near the hut where he was found. Strangely enough the incident seems to have quelled the antagonism and the subject of sabotage doesn't come up, although deep down everyone knows that Subby must be the culprit. He had the know-how, and now we know that he had a motive, however twisted. Everyone is anxious to get back to normal, and shake off the stigma of what has taken place.

'The facts,' states Welks in one isolated outburst, 'are obvious. Subby was a gutless bastard who just could not face up to the job. When the heat got too great he broke.'

The wardroom is only the thickness of a metal screen away, and everyone, including myself, holds his breath to listen.

'More interested in flowers than sailoring,' goes on the nasal voice. 'Soft as shit with his namby pamby ways. I'll bet there is a whole army of doting aunties waiting to weep for him back home.'

I hear a movement and a curt, 'Excuse me,' from the navigator. When I go out into the passage and look into the wardroom Welks is seated alone, with a whisky held halfway to his lips. Two other half-filled glasses stand on the green baize in mute condemnation. I see no cause to hold back.

'You haven't changed a bit, have you?' I snarl into his face. 'Subby was worth ten of you, and I reckon that your new messmates are beginning to learn the truth.'

He rises as far as the lip of the table allows. 'You can't talk to me like this! You're in the rattle, Grant. This time I'll see the book thrown at you for speaking to me like this.'

I don't want to hear the end of it as I climb up through the conning-tower into the sunshine. There is a queer feel to the weather now. Humid, clammy and oppressive. Even the breeze that sweeps in from the sea is unpleasantly warm and sultry. Later on the typhoon warning comes, and like the rest of the Fleet *Audacity* is ordered to sea. Better to ride out the storm than risk breaking loose from moorings in a crowded anchorage.

VI

You would have thought that the typhoon was sent by divine providence for the benefit of our captain. We head out of Hong Kong with everything battened down and well secured, while everyone on the bridge wears heavy-weather harness. Studding rides the bridge as though it is a chariot, challenging the wind as it hurls in out of the east to batter the boat with its malicious strength. We shut the upper lid and use the engine inductors, and the crew sits in its own sweat as the humidity builds up.

Hardened seamen are rendered speechless by the sheer ferocity of the storm. *Audacity* bucks and heaves continuously, with a third of her length lifting clear at times before she see-saws to thump down into a trough and bury her snout deep into the solid mass of water that rears up on the other side of the gulf. As far as the eye can see the surface is a ridged, moving body of spuming foam. Spray fifty feet high hurtles in to lash at the faces of those who stand lookout, and it is like staring into a sand-blaster. There is a horizontal shroud of driving mist sweeping across the surface as the wind whips the crests off the waves and shreds them into a frothy veil. Huge rollers rise out of the ocean and hang like concave cliffs before crashing down to swamp the whole boat. It is as though a monster as big as the Universe is snorting at us with its super-heated breath, and some maniacal organist has found a chord to send the fear of God through us, and keeps his fingers pressed on the keyboard to build up a screaming, discordant howl.

To look at the storm for more than a few seconds is to have your face blasted raw by the rasping needles of spray, and binoculars are utterly useless in this wilderness of driving waste. The radar screen is blotched with wave-clutter as pulses of energy bounce back from huge bodies of moving water.

Inside the hull the stores we stowed so meticulously are jerked out of their lodgings to go tumbling through the boat, evading the futile efforts of the men who spend half their time airborne and the other half clinging on to stop themselves being thrown against the sides by the wild movements of the boat. The helmsman strives to anticipate what she will do next as she careers about, and it is an achievement to keep within seven degrees of the ordered course, when at times the rudder lifts clear as she pivots on the ridge of a swell. We hold our breath while she makes up her mind which way to fall, and when she does seesaw she plummets down with a force that knocks the breath out of our bodies. A thousand poltergeists hurtle through the hull, plucking out everything that is not fastened down and throwing it in all directions.

Only one man relishes the insanity of it all as he remains on the bridge for hours on end, as though he is reluctant to go below in case the wind will ease if he is not there to urge it on. He roars with laughter when the navigator reports gusts exceeding one hundred and fifty miles per hour.

As night falls it seems to increase the nightmarish quality of it. The diesels struggle with the ever-changing pressure on the screws as she lifts them free from the restraining clutch of the sea, or dips them deep into the restricting pressures below as her bow soars like a condemning finger, with white water gushing from every aperture. Invisible entrails of spuming surf leap in out of the darkness to smash into our exposed faces, and it is impossible to anticipate the vicious talons that are determined to rip us apart. It is enough just to hang on and try to peer out into the black mass that envelops her, hoping that any other vessel in the vicinity will have a bridge high enough to allow her lookouts to keep their glasses dry, and catch sight of our low profile before they run us down. Our running lights look weak and impotent as they blink out into the storm like the eyes of some small animal alone in the dark.

I am kept busy patching cuts and abrasions, and as dawn comes we get our first indication that the worst is over. The ocean no longer steams with a constant shroud of vapour and there is a rhythm in *Audacity's* movements. By mid-morning of the second day we see the sun again, and the men set about dumping the ruined stores and securing what remains. Normal routine takes over and I am given Subby's watch to do, on the strict understanding that I make no decisions on my own, and call the captain at the least sign of trouble.

Studding sets our course northwards towards the Straits of Formosa and holds it there even when the sea is eased enough to allow us to turn back to Hong Kong as everyone expects. It is assumed that there must be an enquiry into Subby's death, and we will have to be there to give evidence, but as the hours go by and the sea quietens to a long swell the boat stays on course, swooping and soaring towards the north with her engines rattling at full speed.

The high cliffs of Japan lift over the horizon as we give way to a two-funnelled ferry with big Japanese characters painted on her hull and a name on her stern that ends with *Maru*. She dips her ensign politely as we head in towards the jaws that make the entrance to Sasebo harbour. Just before I go below to take the wheel a cold hand grips my inside as I notice the small boom-defence vessel dragging aside the anti-submarine nets to allow us through. This is the first real tangible sign of war I have seen, and it hits home like a punch below the belt. I had cheered and revelled with the rest when VE day arrived. It was the promise of lasting peace, and the whole world, including the Russians and her satellites, would work together for a decent future for everyone. Yet, here we are five years on, entering a strange anchorage where a grim armada of ships swing at their moorings with all the paraphernalia of war blatantly exposed. We secure alongside a Royal Fleet Auxiliary tanker and begin to suckle from her and take on stores. The men must work throughout the night to replenish, for there is an air of urgency about the place.

Only when the boat is fully serviced and ready for war am I allowed to spread the word that the port watch is to receive liberty. A small landing craft is placed at our disposal and I go ashore with the first batch.

I stand with the coxswain on his small platform on the starboard side as we putter in towards the town past the huge bulk of the US carrier *Valley Forge* that dominates the scene. The smaller *Neptune* looks strangely innocuous in her lighter shade of grey as she rides at her buoy with a gaggle of supply craft nestling against her flank like suckling piglets. Cruisers, destroyers, landing craft, and all types of war vessels make up the bulk of a huge invasion fleet preparing for battle. They come from many parts of the world, although the predominant mass is from the United States, and it all looks grimly ominous as we glide by, threading through a stream of small fishing boats with stove-pipe exhausts puffing into the still air to the echoing pulse of their engines. Bland Japanese faces peer back at us; subdued and self-effacing, and some even bow when we come near, bringing a deep sense of resentful anger boiling up inside me as I recall the way they purged South-East Asia with unbridled cruelty. I find their gestures of humiliation almost as repellent as their arrogant bestiality and fanaticism when they thought themselves invincible disciples of a divine empire.

We pass a side creek that leads away to port, and the coxswain tells me that he lands officers there at times. It is a scene from an old Japanese print, with terraced gardens rising to the tree-lined cliffs, criss-crossed by zig-zagging paths with shrines and a pagoda standing amongst a profusion of fairy-tale flowers, shrubs and foliage. It is ablaze with colour, and looks as though every individual flower leaf and branch has been carefully arranged.

A Capful of Glory

When I step ashore in Sasebo there is a sort of festive holiday in process, and dainty, ornately-kimonoed women mince along, some with babies strapped to their backs, while well-behaved, docile children play in groups in floral *Mikado* costumes and short, jet-black hair: Sexless, impossibly angelic, with easy smiles always at the ready.

I find it hard to reconcile all this chintzy frippery with the evidence of what we saw in Singapore and in news-reels. Impossible to compare the people who compose these immaculate gardens and fine, eggshell crockery, with the beasts who rampaged through occupied countries, performing atrocities that could only be conceived by twisted minds.

'It's false!' my mind cries out angrily. 'This smiling Japanese print with its blatant charm and coquettish beauty is a con. No nation can change so abruptly. These little men shuffling along in soft shoes with separate compartments for their big toes are the same as those who tortured and raped their way through the Far East.'

Yet you cannot stay angry for long with a docile, subjugated, fairyland mob like this, who go out of their way to show how humiliated they are. I have seen pictures of emaciated British troops with their running sores and broken bodies. Heard about the thousands who died building a railway to nowhere, and cringed at the horrific stories of cruelty and deprivation; but already the images are fading. For me and others who were not directly involved it is impossible to sustain those flint-sharp memories. Our senses are dulled by repetitive visions that came from a far off land, and we are awakening from a nightmare that sickened our minds and saturated our brains with an over-abundance of bestiality.

It has nothing to do with forgiveness or an acceptance that these people were carried along on a wave that allowed no compromise. Two atom bombs have not evened the score. It is just that it is pointless to keep reminding ourselves of it.

For a while I wander aimlessly along a street lined with hundreds of streetlamps and telegraph poles standing in front of flat-fronted buildings with blatant advertising boards. Perhaps because it is a holiday only one small, square, black car squats alongside the kerb, and a few desultory bicycles meander along the patched tarmac. Ahead of me the barren shoulders of a ridge of hills rise into the sky.

It is a strange mixture of old and new: a blatant contrast between Japanese culture and banal, modern, urban development that is entirely lost to me as I loiter on a corner, watching a couple of young matelots having their portraits etched by a street artist. His easel is set up in the road oblivious of passing cyclists or the occasional vehicle that comes along.

'You okay?'

A bronzed, pugnacious face with a crumpled peaked cap pushed back from creased eyebrows peers in at me. On his shoulders the PO wears flashes that tell me he is from Canada, so I assume he is from one of the sleek, dark, destroyers with names like *Sioux*, *Athabaskan* and *Cayuga* that are moored in pairs between the bigger ships.

'You look lost, buddy,' he says when I stare back vaguely.

'I'm okay,' I respond carefully, suspicious of people who accost others out of the blue like this. 'Just getting the feel of the place.'

'You won't do that standing here.' He has a proprietorial air about him as he allows his eyes to sweep across the scene. 'This is just the icing; you ought to meet the people.'

'Should I?' I can't help liking the bloke, but there is something not quite right about being picked up off the street by a stranger.

He seems to read my thoughts. 'I wondered if you was off the carrier. A whole gang of us had a wow of a time with some of their guys last night.'

I shake my head. 'No.'

His mouth tightens and some of the mirth goes out of his

face. 'Look, buddy. If you don't wanna talk that's your business. I was just trying to be matey. We are all in this together, you know.'

I relent. 'Sorry, mate. You caught me off-guard. I can't get used to being amongst the Japs like this.'

He nods slowly. 'Yeah, I know what you mean.' He looks about him in silence, as though making up his mind about something. 'How'd you like to meet a family?' he asks eventually.

'I don't know.' The caution is back in my voice.

'Oh I don't mean a whore-house. You want to stay well clear of those. Only the Japs themselves know the genuine geisha houses. What's left is not always disease-free.'

'I'm not in the mood.'

'Don't make up your mind until you see what's on offer. There are things about the way of life out here that takes a bit of getting used to. Just come along with me and see the genuine article.' He makes the 'i' in 'genuine' sound like wine.

So, because I don't know what else to do, I follow him into a side-street. He walks straight up to a door, winks at me, and opens it without knocking. Inside there is a cross passage that stretches the whole width of the building where he slips off his shoes and tells me to do the same. After that he slides back half a wall, made from floral patterned paper, to reveal a large room that is bare except for a big, circular quilt that covers most of the floor, with a charcoal burner sticking out of its centre. We are greeted with bows and back-shuffles by an elderly Jap and his wife, and they invite us to squat with our legs beneath the edge of the quilt while 'mamasan' serves tea in delicate porcelein bowls, and 'papasan' waits patiently on the fringe.

When the silence has gone on long enough I ask. 'How did you find this place?'

He laughs. 'I didn't. They found me. I left my mates and strolled off on my own, just like you. I guess I must have looked a bit more subdued than the rest 'cause the old guy's daughter came right up out of nowhere and invited me here.' He hesitates when he sees the look on my face. 'You needn't look like that. They ain't whores; least, not the way you think.'

'They?'

'Oh, didn't I say? There's two of them. I tell you, buddy they are like china dolls! Soft as velvet.'

My face hardens. 'I said I wasn't interested.'

He sighs. 'Nobody's forcing you, but I've bin given the run of the joint and they can't do enough for me. It seems a shame to let it go to waste. Right now the family is struggling to make a living. It's a strange set-up. They won't accept something for nothing, and it is getting downright embarrassing on my own. Most of the guys I know wouldn't treat the place right. You look like a man who knows how to behave, and that's why I brought you along.'

I am not convinced, and I'm half inclined to shove off and leave him to it. I am about to get up when two girls come in. The tallest is five feet nothing and looks slightly less childlike than the kids I saw on the jetty. The other looks even younger.

'They're kids!'

'Don't believe it. That's how they are out here. Rosie speaks English a bit, don't you, gal? She will tell you they're over sixteen.'

'Rosie! That's a good Japanese name.'

'Yeah, well I couldn't get my tongue round their real ones, so I call the tallest Rosie and the other Princess. She's the one I'm stuck on.'

'I see.' I look at Rosie. She is slim and graceful as she looks at me with a half-smile, and lowers her eyes demurely when she sees my stare. Mamasan serves a second cup of saki, and it filters through, warming me and taking away my doubts. Two more and my resolution is dented. The Canadian is blowing smoke rings thoughtfully as he watches me dissolve. He knows exactly the right moment to slip his legs out from under the quilt and go off with Princess, through an inner sliding door. Before he disappears he turns. 'You comin'?'

Half an hour later we are lying back, quietly contemplating the ceiling. She was warm, soft and therapeutic. There was something mechanical about the whole thing, yet it was completely satisfying. I feel as though I have been part of a business deal, and I could put her back on the shelf now that I have had my money's worth. Then she spoils it all by showing that she has a brain.

'Japanese soldier good soldier – yes?'

Her voice startles me, and I look at the Canadian.

He chuckles quietly. 'She's different to the rest: always asking awkward questions.'

'Japanese soldier make to die – not make to take prisoner,' she insists, staring into my eyes.

'There's no virtue in dying,' I snap grimly; then seeing the vague look in her face I explain slowly, 'Better to live for Japan. You are no bloody use to anyone dead.'

She thinks about that for a moment, then smiles a crafty, elfin smile. There is a cold, calculating expression in her eyes. A half concealed repugnance that makes me feel dirty. 'You do not make to die for England?' She looks away with her mouth slightly twisted. 'Japanese have honour. It is like opium to him.'

I stare down at her. Maybe she is the beginning of a new generation who will throw off the shame heaped on her by her forebears. I jerk round as the door suddenly slides open. A young man's face peers in, and immediately both girls crawl out of the sheets and dress quickly, without another word.

After they have gone the Canadian chortles. 'Can't figure it out, can you? I told you things are different out here. That's the guy Rosie is gonna marry. You are part of her dowry.'

He is pulling on his pants, but stops when he sees my expression. 'What's bitin' you, for Christ's sake! It's the way they are, I tell you, if it had not bin you it would have bin someone else. Don't you feel better for it?'

Outside in the alleyway a group of kids are playing. They stop their game and look up with their enigmatic smiles, and I glower back at them. The smiles fade. Their faces look anxious and hurt. 'Damn the lot of you!' I grate aloud at them. 'All you ever do is smile.'

The Canadian is hurrying to catch up. 'Just wait 'til you meet the Koreans. You'll really wonder what the hell you've gotten yourself into.'

I search his grinning face. 'You been there?'

'We picked up some marines from Pusan.' He shakes his head knowingly, 'It's a god-damned police state – almost as bad as the Nazis. Anyone who doesn't toe the line – zup!' He draws a finger across his throat. Nobody gets to talk against the government. First thing you notice when you get out of the town is the stink. Koreans throw nothing away; not even their own shit. The nightsoil is taken out to the fields in leaky old tanks and spread round to make the crops grow, and the villages have open sewers running right down the middle of what passes for the main street. You can't get away from that stench no-place. If I live to be a hundred that's what Korea will always mean to me – a bloody awful stink.'

We walk in silence. At the landing a mass of liberty boats and small landing craft jockey for position to take off their quota of men. Yanky Whalers with clanging bells and animated coxswains. Huge launches with enough room for an army that pivot in their own length as they try to avoid each other, and a host of other craft. The noise is incredible as shore-patrolmen batter luckless shipmates at the slightest provocation, imagined or otherwise. Close to me a man heaves his guts into the black water.

Somehow, amidst the bedlam we locate a destroyer's cutter and bum a lift from its friendly coxswain who agrees to drop me off at the tanker. It is dark and cold as we swing out into the creek and begin to putter towards the ships, leaving the blasphemous noise astern. A two-way procession of ship's boats fill the night with the roar of engines, and

I am glad to reach the sanctity of *Audacity,* with her muttering diesels and pulsing fuel-lines.

My feet hardly touch the deck of the fore-ends when I find the navigator standing beside me. 'We have been waiting for you to return, Grant. The captain's holding a meeting, and you are to attend. The tanker's captain has kindly loaned us the wheelhouse so that we can have space and privacy.'

We assemble like ghosts in the big wheelhouse and push the doors shut. I am the only NCO present, and the Merchant Navy leaves us strictly alone while we talk. When Studding enters he wastes no time in getting down to business, and spreads a couple of charts on the table before nodding us into a tight circle. I stand respectfully in the background, but even from here I can read what it says on the charts. 'Bo Hai, and the northern part of the Yellow Sea,' says one, while the other reads, 'Ping Yong Inlet' with a small insert 'Chinnampo Ko.'

'You may be wondering why I have included Grant in this gathering,' he begins. 'So, it gives me great pleasure to make a small announcement before we start. All sorts of innovations are taking place at Gosport, and new submarines are on the way. There is even a rumour about a boat that can stay submerged indefinitely – but I'll believe that when I see it. However, apart from that, the whole training programme is to become more sophisticated, and we are even going to have a one hundred foot escape tank. Grant is being offered an appointment with the people who are setting the whole thing up, and it carries with it a promotion to lieutenant. I'm sure you will wish to join me in congratulating him.'

I am stunned into silence as they gather round to shake my hand. I accept Welks' limp mauler and try to ignore the contempt in his eyes, but the others are genuine enough.

'The bastard!' I am thinking as I look at Studding's smug face. 'So much for confidentiality!' For a moment I am on the point of throwing it back in his face and telling him that I have no intention of accepting a commission, but the notion dies quickly. For one thing, I haven't the will or the guts, and for another, I am secretly pleased that it has all finally come out. I have wrestled with the problem for so long it is a relief to have the decision made for me, even under these circumstances. So, when it comes to shaking his hand I grip it with enthusiasm. I am committed now. My future has been fixed; and I am glad.

'Right, gentlemen,' states Studding firmly. 'With that done I can bring your suspense to an end by telling you where we are bound, and what lies in store for *Audacity*. I have argued long and hard for this opportunity to prove ourselves, and there is many a senior officer who believes we have bitten off more than we can chew. It is up to us to make them swallow their doubts.'

He moves across to the charts and spreads his hands on the surface. 'You cannot have failed to notice all the activity going on here, and you must realise that something big is going on. I can tell you that General Douglas MacArthur has put forward an audacious, imaginative plan to make a landing at Inchon. It will take the enemy in the rear and probably shorten the war if it succeeds.'

He jabs a finger at the chart. 'This is Inchon. On the fifteenth September – three days from now, two hundred and thirty ships are due to take part in the landing. They have even requisitioned landing craft that were handed over to the Japanese to replace civilian ferries, along with their crews, so you can see what a vast operation it is. Normally a landing of this scale would take something like sixty days to plan. This one has been put together in little over a fortnight. The area is extremely tidal, and at high water the sea laps over the wall, while at low water there are mud-flats everywhere. In fact it is just about the worst place you could pick for a landing, if you had a choice.'

He waits to allow his words to sink in before going on in a deadly serious voice. 'To confuse the North Koreans, several mock landings and bombardments are taking place even now on different parts of the coast. Am I boring you, Mr Welks?'

For a second Welks's eyes stay glazed, then he jolts back into reality. 'No – er – no, sir. It's just that charts mean very little to me, and I cannot see what all this has to do with my end of the boat.'

Studding grits his teeth. 'Don't you now. Well, you are not isolated from the rest of us, so pay attention and you might learn something.'

He goes back to the chart. 'All this is only background to our little enterprise, but it will allow us to slip by unnoticed when we sail up the west coast of Korea, and in some ways our mission could have just as far-reaching effects on the war effort as the Inchon landings.'

Once again he allows his words to sink in. 'Some believe that MacArthur should stop at the Thirty-Eighth Parallel, but that he is a glory-seeker who intends to push on to the Yalu River and the borders of China. They argue that in doing so he will invite retaliation from either the Russians or the Chinese. Others think that a couple of well-placed atomic bombs would settle the matter quickly and decisively. I do not need to tell you how alarmed that makes some of our politicians. However, I don't think that is a serious proposition ... I'd be obliged if you would pay attention, Chief.'

Once again Welks jerks upright. 'Sorry, sir, I still can't see what this has to do with us.'

'I am coming to that if you have patience. What concerns some politicians is the threat of full-scale, global war. Once MacArthur has begun his advance he may not know when to stop.' He smirks derisively. 'My own opinion is that he should drive the North Koreans right off the map. I don't believe that we have anything to fear from a lot of ill-equipped Chinese peasants who have their hands full with Chiang-Kai-Shek.'

He turns away from the chart and takes a moment to look into our faces. 'There have been vague and unconfirmed reports of the Chinese massing on the border. Unfortunately our aircraft have strict orders not to fly across the Yalu River, so reconnaissance flights are out. Therefore, two South Korean officers have volunteered to infiltrate the north and find out if there is any substance to the rumours. They were parachuted in four days ago, and although they do not anticipate any real problems moving about the countryside, it is virtually impossible to return through enemy lines. So, it is our job to pick them up and bring them home.'

He thumps a fist into his other palm and twists it hard. 'The ROK officers will make their way by sampan to a small island called Seki-To, near the mouth of the Ping Yang Inlet. At the northern tip is a much smaller islet called Shimai-To with a lighthouse, uninhabited, except for the keepers.

'We will rendezvous there at high tide, approximately seventeen hundred hours on the fifteenth, while the main landings at Inchon are taking place. One mile west of Shamai-To there is fifteen fathoms of water with a shingle and shale bottom. If we take care we can find a nice spot on which to sit throughout the day. The initial landings are due to take place on Wolmi-Do Island on the morning tide. So, hopefully, the North Koreans will have their hands full while we sneak into the area. All we have to do is sit and wait for nightfall.'

He sways back and grins. 'There it is, gentlemen. You could have a hand in shaping the war if we pull it off.' He looks at me. 'There could even be a couple of medals, and that wouldn't go amiss for someone with your ambitions, Grant.'

His smile fades. 'What is biting you, Pilot? You look as though you have swallowed a toad.'

The navigator leans forwards with a grim expression on his sad face. 'I have studied that area, sir. It is not submarine country, is it? It would be much wiser to choose Cho To for the pick-up. It too has a lighthouse, and we would not need to negotiate the only navigable channel through the shoals. What I am saying is, surely the North Koreans will have that fairway well defended.'

Studding's face takes on an impatient expression. 'The "gooks" will be busy, Pilot. In any case it would have been impossible for the two officers to get to Cho To.' He smiles magnanimously. 'Anyway, it will be a test of your skills, and I would have thought the challenge would excite you.'

The navigator moves across to the chart-table and points a long, bony finger at the channel just north of Cho To. 'That is what concerns me, sir. The soundings come right down to nine fathoms in some places. Fifty-four feet. We will have to go in at periscope depth, or risk running aground. Even then, at thirty-seven feet there will be little water under the keel. If they have listening devices set up they could trap us easily, and any prowling aircraft would have us at its mercy.'

'Not at night it won't,' insists Studding.

'At night!' The navigator is aghast. 'What happens if the enemy switches off the navigation lights?'

'One light is all we require. The fairway lies between the northern tip of Cho To to the light on Seki To. It won't be the first time a submarine has crept into a strange landfall by moonlight. The two ROK officers will make certain that we do have a light of some kind. Damn it, man, we can't expect to have it laid out on a plate for us!'

The navigator refuses to be brow-beaten. He is an uncomplicated bloke, without a lot of imagination or ambition; but he is immensely proud of his expertise. 'With due respect, sir. It is my duty to bring your attention to navigational hazards.'

'All right!' snorts Studding. 'Your objections have been noted. Now: do you think we can get on with it?'

He is upset. The unquestioning loyalty he normally expects is missing, and even his own officers are placing obstacles in his way. His mouth tightens determinedly. 'The boat will go to Harbour Stations in one hour. As soon as we are at sea I will tell the ship's company what we are about. Perhaps then I will see some of *Audacity's* spirit come to the surface.' He gathers up the charts and stalks out in high dudgeon.

'I didn't think he would take it like that,' complains the navigator. 'It is my job, after all.'

'Don't let it worry you, Pilot,' advises Tyson cheerfully. 'It is an anxious time for the captain. He was looking for support, and although your comments needed to be said, they were hardly welcome. Once we get to sea you will soon see a change in him.'

'Bloody glory hunter!' Welks' griping voice snaps our heads round. He is standing slightly apart from us, with his glowering eyes and surly features infused. 'I would like to know how much of all this stems from his craving for glory.'

'Careful what you say,' warns Tyson angrily. 'I won't listen to criticism of the captain.'

'Of course not!' sneers Welks. 'I am supposed to stand back and listen to you death or glory boys planning how best to earn your medals; then go below and get my lads to turn to, and the machinery running. My men have been accused and abused by the deck brigade, only to find that it was one of the Dartmouth club who tried to wreck the boat.'

He rounds on me. 'I earned my stripe, Grant. You are being offered yours on a plate. Well, just remember this. Me and my grease-monkeys are not here for the benefit of dabtoe medal-chasers. You are not going to ride to glory on our backs.'

'That's enough!' barks Tyson. 'I have heard enough of your bloody nonsense. Any further remarks and you'll find yourself in serious trouble.'

The engineer's face contorts. 'Go on then,' he raves. 'Tell the captain what I've said. The boat is short-handed already. If he carries on like this he won't have enough crew left to do the job at all.'

We can only stare in amazement as he rants at us. These emotions must have been pent up for some time, and now there is no stopping him. His eyes are wild as he raves on. 'We are treated like dummies by our illustrious captain. He doesn't give a damn for anyone but himself. If he doesn't start treating my blokes properly he can't expect a full whack from them: They are not bloody robots!'

He is choking over his words as he goes on. 'I won't guarantee that they will work their guts out anymore. You 'ad your say, Pilot, and he wouldn't listen to you. I was not even allowed to say my piece. We have worked like stink to keep the boat running, despite the efforts of one of your lot, but my lads are getting sick of picking up the pieces while the seamen get all the cream. I am giving you the message loud and clear: don't push us too far!' He chokes to a stop, and we are shocked into silence.

'I think you are over-tired, Mr Welks,' says Tyson in a steady voice. 'I advise you to go away and think about things before you say anymore. I have taken note of your concern for the well-being of your men and I will mention it to the captain at the appropriate time. However,' he adds quickly when Welks seems about to begin again, 'for your own good I suggest you get your thoughts in order. Despite what you may believe, everyone is aware of the fine work your men are doing. Perhaps we do not tell you often enough.'

Welks has blown himself out. His face has collapsed as he digests Tyson's words. There is nothing left in him now, and when I slide open the door he sidles out without another word.

I receive some peculiar looks from the crew when I get back inside the boat. They know full well that something special is going on, and no doubt the 'buzz merchants' are spreading rumours about with wild imagination. Most men keep their thoughts bottled up and go about their duties quietly, and when I wander aft I find none of the dissension that Welks raved about. In fact, there is a new feeling now that the long days of boredom are over and it looks as though we are finally going to do something positive. The only exception is Leading Signalman Thorpe, and we are all getting used to his miserable face by now. My efforts to revive him ceased long ago, for it is like battering against a brick wall.

My new Harbour Station is on the casing with the berthing party. Like Subby before me I am in nominal charge, but Dinger Bell and his men could do their work blindfolded and need no one to tell them what to do. The gunlayer is in charge aft, and his men have already singled-up the hawsers before I arrive. I am there only to take ultimate responsibility when things go wrong.

Studding insists on the casing-party wearing clean sweaters for the occasion, and once the gear is stowed away they line up, tallest forward – shortest aft as we glide past the grey ships. First comes *Neptune,* and her sailors come to attention as they turn to face us when the strident notes of her bugle responds to the thin whistle of our bos'n's call. She looks big and powerful with her Sea Furys and Fireflys ranged on the flightdeck. After that we exchange salutes with an assortment of other warships until we run clear and head for the little boom-defence vessel.

We slide out through the gap, and it is time to dismiss the casing-party, except for Bell: who must inspect the wires and ropes with me to ensure that they are well stowed before we hit the open sea.

Just to complicate matters a second typhoon moves into the Tsushima Strait, ready to make life miserable for the invasion troops in their flat-bottomed craft. *Audacity* takes it all in her stride; rattling along half-buried at times, and shaking tons of white water from her back when she rises to swoop over the crests. We lose the full force of it when we turn into the Yellow Sea after rounding the island of Cheju-Do, with about five hundred miles to go. Our engines pound away as though they are eager to reach the war, but it will take another thirty hours to sail up the west coast of Korea and on through the one hundred mile wide neck that lies between Shantung on mainland China and the Onjin peninsula.

The sea turns a murky green as we leave the typhoon astern, and there is a greyness about the cold sky and empty wilderness of sea. The cold bites into my bones as I stand my watch on the bridge: All the more pronounced because we have so recently sweltered in the tropics. Thin veils of snow drift in to stick to the metal standards, and increase the jumping-wire to the diametre of a man's arm before the vibration of the engines shakes it free to fall with dull plopping sounds onto the casing.

I lose my taste for its naked beauty and bury my chin into the damp warmth of my duffle-coat, pulling the hood over my woollen hat against the vicious wind. Occasionally we catch a glimpse of another ship labouring along. Always grey like us, and always heading north, with a stuttering signal lamp asking who we are, or responding to our own challenge.

We hear the distant rumble of gunfire heavy to the west, reminding us that twenty miles or so to starboard a war is going on. There is tension out here, but it is numbed by the long hours of boredom, for we are remote from the battle, with no obvious purpose to our progress. Lookout relieves lookout with the bare minimum of words, reporting their relief to the officer of the watch, and asking permission to go below into the muggy warmth. They have to be reminded to stay vigilant, for the menace is closing in on either side as we head for the narrows. The unrelieved pewter sky presses down on us with heavy banks of cloud and the whole scene has the quality of stygian gloom. It is a sullen, forbidding world up here.

When Studding tells us what we are about everyone listens with stoic calm. He skips the finer details and makes no mention of the navigational hazzards that lie ahead. His tone is flat and uninspiring. As far as he is concerned we are going to do a job, and anyone who fouls things up, or shows less than excellence will face his wrath. Gone are the fire-eating speeches. Now it is all threat and grim warning for anyone who falls below par.

VII

Just before dawn on the fifteenth of September *Audacity* slides down through the murky depths to settle on a mixture of sand and shingle, and her crew take up their positions without fuss, while one hundred and fifty miles to the south-west marines are already moving in towards 'Green Beach' on the island of Wolmi-Do.

It squats across the entrance to the tidal basin of Inchon harbour, and two days ago, at half past noon, four cruisers and six destroyers began to bombard the area. The North Koreans responded with their 75mm guns, and inflicted slight damage to some of the destroyers which had closed in to within six miles. Yesterday they switched target to the town of Inchon itself and began again, with air support from carrier-based aircraft.

The marines found little resistance at first. By oh eight double oh, while we sit quietly eating breakfast in ninety feet of water, the commander of the Third Battalion, Fifth Marines reports that the island is secured, and his total casualties number seventeen wounded and no dead. Right now tanks with bulldozer blades are busy burying alive the few stubborn North Koreans still hiding underground. General MacArthur's gamble is paying off.

A glance at the chart tells me that we are about five miles due west of Shimao-To (Sister island), where a neat notation is printed to warn mariners to use extreme caution in the approaches because of extensive shoaling in the area.

Our hydrophone operators concentrate with their headphones, listening for the sound of surface craft, well aware that any traffic in our vicinity consists mostly of junks under sail, with only the creak of timber or the squeal of rudder pintles to give away their position.

We sit in cramped silence, conserving energy and air in the stagnating atmosphere, trying to ignore the clock, for the hands move agonisingly slowly as each interminable second ticks by. There is a strange lack of tension in the boat, and some of the older hands with years of war experience find it difficult to take things seriously, and not treat it like some over-elaborate exercise. It seems impossible that just beyond the horizon men are being maimed and killed: that we are surrounded on three sides by hostile forces. No one really expects a brace of destroyers to come racing out with their sonar pinging and their racks full of primed depth-charges. Now and again a swirl of water through the casing above our heads reminds us of where we are, but in all other respects it could be a normal 'make and mend.'

The United Nations forces have almost total command of the air, and only the footslogging troops moving through the stinking fields, or rooting out the enemy in the streets know what a real war this is. Now and again Studding lifts us off the bottom and takes us up slowly to periscope depth for a look round. Those of us who are near enough watch his face while he crouches with his eyes at the lenses, but he makes no sign and tells us nothing. The boat settles back to the bottom again and we wait for darkness to come. I have not thought of Zoe for several days; being fully occupied with coming to terms with my new duties. I have had a crash course on the 'fruit machine' from Tyson, for it will be me who feeds data into the small computer in the unlikely event of a torpedo attack, while the skipper relays them from the periscope. The attack team consists of him, Thorpe reading the bearings whenever he calls 'mark.' The navigator plotting the whole thing on his chart. Tyson keeping control of the boat, and me doing Subby's old job on the firing panel. In his corner the controlroom log keeper will note every order as it is passed. It is a well-tested and tried formula, but no one really believes we will be using it, even though our torpedoes are fitted with war-heads.

At dusk we go to 'diving stations' again so that Studding can take us up for a final look before it goes dark. The ERA on the diving-panel feeds air slowly into the tanks until she lifts upright with a slight judder and floats gently off the sea-bed. The motors whine in response to the telegraphs and we ascend like a big fish with the two men on the hydroplanes carefully controlling the rate at which we climb with a nice easy angle.

As the needles rotate towards thirty-seven feet I am watching Studding's face as he waits to signal for the periscope. He bends to meet the eye-pieces as they emerge from the well, snapping down the handles; and I see the first gleam of daylight reflect in his eyes as it breaks surface surface. He 'walks' the 'scope round, backheeling a full circle until he stops suddenly with his jaw dropping open.

'Down 'scope – half ahead together – eighty feet!'

The hydroplane indicators go to 'hard dive,' and the needles on the depth gauges revolve slowly clockwise. Every unoccupied pair of eyes focus on Studding's face as he jerks back from the eyepieces to stand with his head slightly bowed and his hands on his hips.

'There is a bloody great junk right up our tail,' he says in a tight voice. 'I don't see how he could miss seeing our periscope.'

We level off at eighty feet. 'How long can I stay on oh three oh, Pilot?'

'No distance I'm afraid, sir. It is three quarter tide or we would already be aground. Better go south-west; say two zero five. It becomes progressively deeper as we go towards Hoki-To.'

'I don't want to wander too far away from our position, but we will have to get clear of that blasted junk. Port fifteen – steady on two zero five!'

The gunlayer repeats the order and the giro ticks over as we circle. Suddenly there is a loud scraping noise along the hull, and a cold hand clamps my stomach. I have never heard that sound before, but I know what it could mean.

'Steady!' warns Studding when he hears the sharp intake of breath. 'I don't think it's mines. My guess is that we have picked up a fishing net. Port ten! Let's see if we can swing the screws clear.'

Our ears are tuned to the stealthy sound as it progresses along the length of the hull. For a moment it seems to have worked clear, then both 'planesmen report simultaneously that they are losing control as the bubbles on their clinometers drift forward to show the stern lifting.

'Group up – full ahead together!' Studding orders, ignoring a look of consternation from Tyson. 'We'll try a little brute force.'

I can feel the angle increasing. The stern must be almost awash now.

'Jesus!' mutters someone. 'We must be towing the bloody thing!'

'Up snort!' shouts Studding, and the ETA reaches up for the control-box. I hear the big ram slide as the snort mast, with its combined exhaust and induction tubes lift into position and the locking pin goes in. I don't like it. The boat is still swimming along with a bow-down angle, and the hydroplanes are having no effect.

Studding has the same worry. 'Blow number one main ballast!' he orders. 'Stand by main engines!'

It seems to be doing the trick. The bow is coming up, but the casing must be showing on the surface. He is hoping to push her clear once we get increased power and speed from the diesels.

'In clutches – full ahead together!'

It is shit or bust time. Welks's men feed compressed air into their engines to turn them over. They choke, stutter, then rumble into life before settling into rhythm.

Now everyone is holding his breath and willing the screws to break us free from the net. I feel the vibration through the soles of my feet, but the angle begins to increase again, becoming more and more acute as the pressure comes on. It is a crazy situation as *Audacity* drags the junk along.

The snort dips beneath the surface, and the float-controlled cut-off valve throttles us. My ears ache with the dropping pressure as the diesels suck a vacuum inside the hull. Some men cry out when the pain comes, for it is an agonising experience. One we have all suffered many times before, and it makes snorting a very unpopular pastime.

This time it is not only a short pause while an errant wave sweeps past. This time the boat is being tilted by the drag on her stern, and unless Studding blows more ballast quickly she is going to nose down to the bottom. I hear him suck in breath to give another order, when the situation is taken right out of his hands as a rising, screeching howl sets our teeth on edge. The excruciating noise grows louder and louder; lifting in pitch until it overpowers all else and pierces our eardrums. It reaches a mind-bending crescendo and cuts off abruptly with a muffled explosion, and the silence that follows is thunderous.

We stand in muted suspense for a moment before Welks bursts into the controlroom, closely followed by Chief Petty Officer Meakin, one of the electricians. Both men are bathed in sweat, and in a disarrayed, wild state, but Welks is a quivering jelly. Wide-eyed, with his face contorted.

'The starboard shaft is seized solid, and sea water has got into the cylinders!' he shouts at Studding, almost grabbing the captain's jacket as he spits out his message. 'I tried to shut down when the load came on, but I was too late!' His breath is wheezing in strained gasps as he pleads.

'Too late my foot!' condemns the electrician. 'I warned you not to start the engines, you incompetent oaf! I warned you it was too bloody late!'

'Silence, both of you!' blares Tyson as *Audacity* hits the seabed with a sickening lurch that throws some people off their feet, then rolls over with a slow, deliberate motion until she settles with a seven degree angle, and slightly down by the bow. For the moment anyway, we are safe.

'Now,' says Studding when all has settled down. 'Let me have a clear report from both of you.'

Both men exchange hate-filled looks, neither anxious to take the lead.

'You first, Welks,' invites Tyson.

The engineer draws a deep breath and gathers himself together. He is having to fight to regain his composure and assemble his words.

'Make it quick, Chief!' barks the captain, just as Welks is about to open his mouth. 'Half the Korean Navy must be alerted by now. God knows what's going on up top! Don't make a saga out of it – just give me the plain, simple facts.'

I notice Tyson raise his eyes in frustration as Studding throws the engineer into confusion again, and my mind flies back to the past. 'This is where we came in.' I'm thinking. My personal feud with Welks began with a fishing trawl wrapped round the screws of another submarine ten years ago in the seas off Norway. Now here he is again, red-faced and spluttering all over the place; a pathetic lump of quivering flesh who has lost control of his department by the sound of it.

'I obeyed telegraphs, sir,' he complains with an anxious whine. 'I shut down the moment I knew we were snagged.'

'Bollocks!' exclaims Meakin derisively. 'I shouted at you to ignore the telegraphs and report that we were in trouble. My starboard motor almost burned out while you were buggering about. If you had allowed me to go astern we might have freed the mess.' He turns to Studding. 'It was already too late, sir. I might have worked the screws free if I could have gone astern before the engine clutches went in.'

'I obeyed orders!' shrieks Welks, and the two men shape up to one another as if they are about to come to blows.

'Stop this bloody nonsense!' roars Studding, stepping between them. 'I haven't got time to waste listening to this. I want a report; not a fiasco!' He rounds on Welks. 'When can I use the engines?'

The engineer gulps hard. 'Not until we have cleared the

screws, sir. The starboard one is seized up solid, and I reckon the net is wrapped round the port one too. If we try to use the engines we will damage them.' He looks away from the skipper's glowering features, and Meakin jerks his head in disgust.

'So!' breathes Studding after a pause. 'It is up to providence.' He turns to Tyson. 'We will have to take her up. There's no future in staying down here.' He looks down at the deck as he speaks his thoughts. 'We will arm a boarding party with Grant in command.'

He grins at the expression on my face. 'Don't be modest, Grant. You've taken over new responsibilities now, and I'm sure you will cope with them. It will be your job to board that stupid junk and take command of it until we can cut ourselves free. With any luck you'll find nothing more than a frightened bunch of fishermen and a ship's cat. I think that if there was anything more aggressive in the vicinity we would have known about it by now.'

He turns back to Tyson. 'Chief EA Cleaver is our best diver. Tell him to get dressed, and to take a second man with him. It should be twilight up there now, and with an overcast sky the gloom will keep us fairly inconspicuous while he does his job. We will just have to pray that the gooks are otherwise occupied.'

He takes a deep breath. 'However, the gun crews will close up at action stations in case we are interrupted. I reckon our four-inch and oerlikon will match anything the locals can come up with if it comes to a stand-up fight.'

The glint is back in his eyes now as he warms to the thought of battle. I must admit that this is when he is at his best, when he has fire in his belly and in an emergency. It seems to clear his brain and concentrate his mind, so that he loses his bombast and becomes reassuringly cool and calculated. 'After all, gentlemen,' he goes on with relish, 'this is a situation for which *Audacity* is most suited. The drills we carried out over and over again could have been designed for it, and we have it down to perfection.'

All the boyish eagerness is there. 'We will do it by the "Studding" book,' he grins. 'Guns and his merry men standing by inside the gun-tower while Grant and his boarding part will be close up to my tail in the conning-tower. I want you over the top and across to that junk before she realises what's hit her. Once you have it under control Cleaver can get to work with the trawl.'

He is positively aglow with excitement, but I see little of his enthusiasm over-flowing onto the others. His inspirational, infectious charisma has deserted him, and the men obey his commands only because he has the authority; not because they wish to please him.

Things move quickly. The old drill takes over as we dress up in our action-working rig and strap on webbing and gaiters. Hancock is my second in command, and he and I arm ourselves with .38 revolvers, while the rest have Lee Enfield .303 rifles. When we are done we all look terribly warlike, and not a little stupid. When we assemble in the control-room we need to stand clear of the magazine hatch, for the gunlayer's men are handling HE shells and magazine drums of .303 for the oerlikon.

One last look round and Studding is about to give the order that will send us scurrying up through the hatch, when, right out of the blue, Tyson puts a dampener on everything by suggesting we wait until it gets properly dark. 'Surely the Koreans will have listening gear, sir? After all, Chinnampo is the main port for their capital, Pyongyang. They could have patrol-boats of some kind, and possible mines and depth-charges. Remember, they are kept well supplied by both the Russians and the Chinese, and probably have a sophisticated armoury.'

'Nonsense!' thunders Studding decidedly. 'A few World War Two tanks and obsolete Yak fighters, that's all. They have shot their bolt, Number One. Exploited their treachery to the full and committed everything to the main thrust in the south. Their only asset is their knowledge of the country and the way they can infiltrate by merging with their own kind. The landing at Inchon is going ahead better than we could have hoped for: They are fully occupied, and won't have time or resources to investigate a slight disturbance offshore. Anyway, I doubt if their whole navy consists of more than a few clapped out patrol boats, and they have neither the skill nor the will to mix it with us.'

Tyson is unconvinced. 'Nonetheless, sir, there are several hours of darkness before we have to make our rendezvous with those ROK officers. Perhaps it would be prudent to wait. After all, the junk could well cut herself free.'

Studding's face goes cold. 'That's right; and tell everyone that we are here. Make no mistake, Number One. If I have to, I will take care of those people up top.'

Tyson looks shocked. 'They are probably only fishermen, sir. They most likely haven't a clue what it is they've latched on to, and scared out of their minds.'

'Perhaps so – perhaps not,' states Studding coldly. 'You have a weird way of looking at things, Andy. Those people are communists. Civilian or not, they are our potential enemy. Damn it, man. Would you have us sit here until kingdom come?'

He straightens his shoulders and takes one find inspection. 'We are going up now while we have them baffled and bewildered, and I intend to make the rendezvous at midnight despite all the adverse advice and comment I am receiving from my so-called lieutenants. Once we are cut loose from that bloody appendage we will make our way into the channel, and right up to the lighthouse. If a U boat can sail into Scapa Flow, sink a battleship, and get back home again, then I am damned sure we can cope with a lot of peasants.'

He faces Tyson for one final thrust. 'One small fishing junk and a lot of whimpering conjecture is not going to deter me. So make up your mind about that, all of you!'

His outburst has stunned us all, and I can see Tyson biting his lip with annoyance, but we have something bigger to concentrate on. The orders are coming in thick and fast and the ERA's fingers are already dancing over the diving panel to send high-pressure air screaming into the ballast tanks. There is nothing for the 'planesmen to do, for without power their controls are useless, and we must allow the boat to find her own attitude when we go up in one quick ascent. Tyson blows his whistle at fifteen feet and I receive half a gallon of Yellow Sea as Studding knocks off the second clip to allow the increased pressure inside the boat to send the hatch crashing back into its clip.

I follow his backside out into the cold air with the others close on my heels. One brief glance is all I get before his insistent voice urges me on over the top. We clamber aft across the band-stand and down onto the after casing, where the steel is slippery and I have to hold on to the jumping wire as I scramble towards the junk. It is hauled up tight against the 'duck's arse' to make it simple to scramble across the tangle of fishing trawl that is draped over the gun'll. There is a lot of shouting going on behind me as I lead my party out onto her deck, and I find myself shouting with them as we surge through a mess of fishing gear that's strewn all over the place.

The grey light is almost faded into night now, but I can see pale, oriental faces peering back at me, full of fear when they see these strange creatures emerging from the steel monster that has risen from the depths. We crowd them back against the break of the poop, and they cringe there while we face them with our weapons held ready.

'Easy!' I shout when one of my lads looks like launching into them. The light has deteriorated into a toneless mixture of sombre shadows, and the air is crisp with frost. Our voices are sharp and resonant when we call to one another. Somewhere a baby cries with a soft, monotonous wailing that merges with the moaning wind and the lazy creak of rigging. Above our head the heavy battened sail droops like a sleeping bat while two guttering oil-lamps cast ghostly halos in a creeping mist.

There is a pungent smell of rotting fish and tar, and when

I grab a halliard to steady myself it feels thick and icy cold with frozen dew. We are holding our guns limp in our hands, feeling rather foolish as our captives stare out with baleful eyes. An old man with a wispy goat-beard and a ridiculous little round hat perched on his head squats studying me with ancient eyes, as though he finds it difficult to tell whether I am human or not. They and their vessel look older than time.

This junk is their home. All they possess is contained within its creaking hull, and we are defiling it with our presence. I can read the anxiety in their eyes; all except the old man's. He just looks bewildered.

The crying stops and yet another pale face appears at the door leading into the living quarters beneath the poop. The mother and I stare at each other as she emerges carefully with her baby clutched tight against her breasts. Here is the first expression that holds no fear, just a look of condemnation that makes me feel ashamed.

'Christ!' growls Hancock. 'Is this Studding's enemy?'

'No, mate,' I breathe as she takes her place beside the others. 'These are people. Stay here and keep an eye on them while I go see if there are any more below.'

'Aye aye, sir!' he snaps derisively. 'I'll see they don't overpower the submarine.' He puts on his best Long John Silver voice. 'Come on ye swabs – lay aft or I'll make ye walk the plank!'

I ignore him and peer into the living quarters. From here they look squalid and thick with the smell of bodies. I haven't the heart to enter so I order a couple of the men to search through the bedding and personal belongings. I know without looking that there is nothing here to concern us, but it must be done, and it feels like raping a bloody cripple as they turn out the pathetic gear.

I am relieved when the men find nothing more lethal than a couple of kitchen knives. Hancock and his blokes have persuaded the Koreans to squat down, and the fear has dissolved a little from their faces. They haven't a clue what's going on, but at least they're quiet, and probably pleased that we are not carving them up. These people have an inborn suspicion of all things military, and know what can happen when soldiers go on the rampage. What's to say that we are any different to those they have seen occupying their land over the years. There are six of them altogether. The old man with the whiskers, the mother and her baby. A small boy, and two young men who squat in one corner watching us with suspicion now they have got rid of their initial fear.

I go to look over the side that rests against *Audacity's* stern. Cleaver has already entered the water, and is settling his mouthpiece in place before giving a thumbs-up and ducking down into the murk. Judging by the state of the trawl he is going to have his work cut out slicing through that lot, for it looks to be a mess of thick, hairy rope and thongs, intertwined like a bunch of bastards. I can imagine it screwed round the prop in a solid chunk.

'Grant!'

The skipper's harsh voice cuts through the thin air and I see him hanging over the side of the bridge staring aft at me.

'Sir?'

'What have you found?'

'Just a family, sir. Nothing to worry about. I doubt if they even know that there's a war on, or whether they are North or South Koreans.'

He grunts something unintelligible, and then goes on. 'We can't afford to hang about. Leave Hancock and couple of hands to watch over them and come inboard. I want to be ready to go as soon as we are free.'

'Aye aye, sir!'

Hancock has heard every word. 'Aye, me hearty!' He bawls through cupped hands as he hops about on one leg. 'I'll give 'em the black spot if they don't behave.' The young boy and the old man are laughing at his antics while some of the others look slightly worried.

I am poised with one foot on the junk's gun'l when,

A Capful of Glory 141

without warning the net tears apart and *Audacity's* stern slumps a couple of feet as we drift away from her. I watch helplessly as the gap grows wider. The wind has got hold of the junk to drive it at a tangent with the big sail frapping uselessly. We must be in a current too, for she is twisting and picking up speed with a whole mess of trawl dangling over her side.

Beneath the poop there is a big steering post standing vertical. I run aft to take hold of it, and feel the kick of the rudder immediately. Within seconds I realise that it works arse about face, and to bring the bow to port I have to push it to starboard. 'Cut the bloody net free!' I yell at Hancock. 'I can't control her like this.'

The Koreans have seen the danger, and the two young men leap into action and begin hacking at the net with hatchets. Our lads join them, dragging the mesh away as it is cut through. Everyone is well aware of the peril as we drift leewards towards a nightmare of shoals and mudflats. Nationality and ideology flies in the wind; if it had ever existed, as everyone concentrates on saving the junk. No man fights better than when his home is under threat, and to these Koreans this is it.

She is really gathering leeway now, and I am struggling to bring her as close up wind as she will go. She is built like a bathtub, with hardly any keel, so I can't afford to take liberties with the wind. If I bring it more than a point or two forward of the beam she takes off sideways as though she is determined to wreck herself.

I pride myself on my sailing. From Montague-rigged whalers to sloop-rigged cutters I always put up a good show when taking exams for promotion and such, and I take more than average interest in it. But this cantankerous old bucket has no respect for naval expertise, and she is giving me a hard time. The Koreans watch, and I admire the way they hide their feelings beneath stoic faces. The two men are much too polite to interfere, and the others manage to keep from laughing outright at my futile efforts.

'Stand by to tack – Ready about.' I shout the orders in my best traditional manner, and Hancock sends his men scurrying about to man the sheets. The rig is simple, and designed to look after itself for the most part. It consists of a huge tackle that rides a 'sailing horse' running athwartships on the poop, and attached to the lower boom of the tattered lugsail. My problem is to bring the whole unwieldy mass of canvas and wood to the windward side of the mast when we go about. It means dipping the leading end of the gaff at precisely the right moment; a task that the Koreans could most likely do in their sleep, but I am finding her every kind of a bitch when I try.

To make matters worse the wind decides that it has had enough for one day and drops dramatically, leaving the sail frapping sullenly between fading gusts. I give up any attempt to sail her, and allow the tide to take her. As though to make me look a complete idiot the current seems to flow away from the shallows and without the conflicting influence of the wind she drifts harmlessly away from danger on her own. For the time being at any rate, we are safe, though *Audacity* is getting further and further away to the south; swallowed up in the night. Studding will need to use his radar to find us when he gets under way again. In the meantime we must sit and wait in the doldrums.

The sharp crack of the four inch jerks me upright, and I stare into the void in time to see the flash of another shot. As far as I can make out *Audacity* is lying stopped between us and the light on Seki-To; or rather Sisters Rock, just off the northern tip of the island.

My mind darts back to the chart. Any ship making for the fairway must find the sector with the fixed white light, then hold it as she runs north to the island. If she strays to starboard the light changes to red, or if she drifts to port it begins to flash white. Somewhere to the south we should see another light on Cho-To, but all I can see is an empty void.

Now comes a flash of another kind, and shortly afterwards I hear the deep thump of gunfire. For a moment I think it is a ship firing at the boat, but then realise that it must come from a shore battery on Seki-To. We hear the shells pass overhead, and I follow their invisible trajectory and pick up the silhouette of *Audacity* when she is lit by another salvo from her gun. She looks to be firing towards the south, away from the shore battery.

'There they are – two of the sods!'

Hancock is pointing a long arm towards the channel, and I can just make out the low shapes of two patrol-boats moving through the murk with their superstructure only faintly visible against the lighter background of the sky.

'The crafty sods are holding their fire,' I growl bitterly. 'They are quite willing to let their army chums cover their approach until they get into position to attack. I'll bet their sterns are loaded with depth-charges.'

'If we can see them, surely the lookouts can,' snorts Hancock as though he is trying to send his thoughts across to the boat.

'She knows there's something out there, but she's got the loom of the land behind them.' I say doubtfully, 'and she's got those shore guns to worry about. If there was only something we could do to help her.'

'Too late, mate. She's seen them. That last shot was on a new angle. I'm sure she's firing at them. Let's hope old Guns is on form today.'

Even as he speaks the two boats roar into life as they throw caution to the wind and open their throttles wide. Now the night is ripped apart as streams of tracer leap out across the sea. The gunners on *Audacity* must be working well, for the barrel is belching flame at regular intervals, while the oerlikon rattles away from the band-stand. Both patrol-boats have huge bow-waves building up as they pour on the power. Their guns are smaller calibered compared to the submarine's, but she is a sitting target as she wallows helplessly in the water, while they can weave about and split her fire. It is all up to the gunners now, and there isn't much sophistication about submarine gunnery; just open-sighted stuff, dependent almost entirely on the skill and imagination of the gun-layer.

I am gripping the bulwark hard-knuckled as the two boats sweep in towards their lame target. *Audacity's* gun barks again, and Hancock thumps my side with excitement when the shell thumps into the side of the leading boat with a brilliant burst of lurid flame that exposes the whole area with its glow as it expands along her entire length.

She swings broadside across the path of her mate, and the helmsman works overtime to take violent avoiding action as a more violent blast consumes the first boat in a ball of fire. She skews out of control, and too late, the other patrol-boat realises she has turned the wrong way. Inevitably she ploughs into the inferno to become part of the conflagration. Ammunition and fuel erupt in a concerted series of explosions that tears the darkness apart and turns night to day.

Our lads are cheering and dancing about on the deck beside themselves as they see the death-throes of the two patrol-boats. One final, all-consuming blast sends a revolving ball of fire soaring into the sky, and some of the falling debris even reaches us, so that we have to kick smouldering ashes over the side before they ignite the dry timbered deck. When the turmoil subsides all that remains is a spreading mess of burning rubbish floating on the surface, and the night begins to close in once more.

The heavy sail thwacks against the mast as the junk leans over to a gust of wind. For a moment I think it is blast from the explosion, but then another bluster rattles the rigging and I realise the wind is making again. This time it is coming from a point that allows me to bring it across the stern and push us out to where the flashes of *Audacity's* four inch is still punching regular holes in the gloom as she switches target to range in on the shore battery.

'I think she is under way,' says Hancock as he peers over my shoulder.

The junk is moving along quite nicely now, for this is all

she is fit for: a soldier's wind to push her gently through the water at a pace that requires patience and forebearance. These people carry their home with them wherever they go, and they see no point on worrying about reaching a destination today, when tomorrow will do just as well. Sailing skills need not be too refined when speed is the last thing on their minds. Even my inept efforts are having results, and I can see that Hancock is right; *Audacity* is moving in a wide circle to bring her bow in our direction. It is easier for her gunners now. They must have been firing almost at the limit of their gun's traverse with the mounting hard up against the training stop.

I don't dare try any fancy stuff as I keep the wind just over my left shoulder to keep the sail pressed nicely against the mast, and the canvas from frapping too much. I don't have too much to be ashamed of neither, for these junk sailors do not care twopence about the finer points. It is enough to keep plodding along at a sensible pace while they get on with the household chores. We are making hardly any leeway as we reach out towards the spot where I saw the flash of *Audacity's* gun.

I get a whiff of the acrid tang of one of the young men as he comes to stand beside me and stare out across the bow. The junk is behaving herself and I am finding it easy to keep her swimming along on course. The lives of these people are regulated by wind and tide and he must have grown up in her, learning all he needs to know about sailoring before he could talk. I nudge his arm and point at the helm, inviting him to take over while I stand aside and watch, and his face lights up with a big grin. If we could understand one another we would hold a conversation: as it is we have a mutual respect and interest in holding course and feeling the wind.

Hancock and a couple of seamen are grouped in the bow, staring ahead into the darkness for the first real sight of *Audacity*. Across the water I can hear the mutter of her diesels as we close in on her, and a hoarse shout from forward brings an immediate response from someone on her casing. Her shape materialises off the starboard bow, and a heaving-line snakes out of the night to land across the shoulders of the waiting men. It is quickly gathered up and hauled in hand over hand until a thicker rope follows.

Without any advice from me the young man brings the junk's head up clear of the submarine's stern and into the wind, until we are drifting sideways in towards her, while the casing party stand by with a couple of fenders in case we thump hard against the ballast tanks. They need not have bothered. The helmsman nurses the junk alongside so gently he would not have crushed an egg, and the heaving line and heavier rope were merely a gesture, for we have more than enough time to jump the small gap as he keeps her tucked against the flat surface of the saddle tank while we leap across. I cast one final look back at her, but already the young man is looking away as he leans the junk into the wind and takes her away into a pool of blackness, where, with hardly a sound, she fades like a ghost ship.

I make my way along the wet casing and up to the bridge where Tyson and the skipper lean over the windbreak together. I suddenly notice that the gun has ceased fire and *Audacity* is wallowing silent and lifeless with her engines shut down. The only sound is the soft slop of her bilges as she rolls easily in the long swell. My brief report is accepted in an off-hand way, as though my part in the affair is of little importance.

The other men are climbing down into the boat, so considering myself dismissed I follow them into an atmosphere of tense scepticism and glum speculation. That rift between the two groups is there again, and they have little confidence in the way the skipper has handled things up to now. There is nothing more demoralising than drifting about aimlessly while the enemy takes pot shots at you from shore batteries only a couple of miles away. Surly comments are being bandied about by some senior hands who should know better, for during my absence confidence has dissolved. They feel that after the skirmish with the patrol-boats our presence is no longer a secret and we should get to hell out of it.

The row between Welks and the electrician has brought a new friction between the men in the engine and motor compartment as each side show their loyalties. The main point of contention is the possible damage to the insulation when the extra load came on after Welks's lack of imagination prevented them from taking emergency action in time. There is a heating and cooling unit designed specially to keep the temperature exactly right, for if it builds up too high the insulation can become seriously damaged, with a risk of fire. Whereas, if the machinery is not kept warmer than the surrounding atmosphere, condensation can occur – with dire results. The port motor took considerable strain when the screw seized up, and the electricians lay the blame squarely on the shoulders of the engineer and his obdurate refusal to see what was happening.

In addition Welks's men are making urgent checks to the diesels to ensure they are in full working order and ready to perform at full speed if required. We have had problems before when the snort was shut down in an emergency. The exhaust valves have become distorted and need constant attention to keep them water-tight, and that's how the sea got into the cylinders when the engine was stopped suddenly. Lately we have avoided shutting down both engines at once, but on this occasion, according to the electricians, Welks panicked. Although the stokers have little affection for their bigoted boss, they side with him when thinly veiled accusations come from their colleagues in the more refined section of the compartment.

I can find nothing to do down here for the moment. It is Solomon's duty now to report any misgivings he might have about the morale. So I ask permission to go up top again, and find the skipper and Tyson still draped over the bridge-rail. The blackness is silent and empty, and a mixed blessing, for although it hides us from our enemies it also means that we cannot call for air support from *Neptune*. The North Koreans know we are here, and by all the accepted rules of combat we should be pulling out into deep water. We have one dodgy motor, the diesels are suspect, and no room to manoeuvre, so a call for help would no doubt bring one of those sleek, Canadian destroyers racing up from Inchon, but even at thirty knots she would take five hours to reach us. Therefore, the sensible thing to do is slip away and lick our wounds. It is what everyone expects – everyone that is, except Studding.

VIII

Studding puts extra lookouts up top with Hancock in charge as he calls yet another meeting in the wardroom. The only officer not present is Welks, and when Tyson suggests sending for him he receives a blunt refusal. 'He has his work cut out in the engine-room, and I am not in the mood for his obstructive comments,' declares the skipper in a tone that implies that unless the engineer has a remarkable change of attitude, or performs a minor miracle with his engines, he is on his way out.

'We have to discuss our next move,' announces Studding, keeping his voice low so that his words do not filter through to the crew. 'Some bloody hope!' I am thinking. 'There are blokes in *Audacity* who are quite capable of picking up a confidential whisper from one end of the boat to the other, and broadcasting it to their mates within seconds.'

'Now that we have missed our rendezvous the expedient thing to do would be to abandon the whole project and sail south again, leaving the ROK officers to find their own way back home.'

'Surely that is our only option, sir,' insists Tyson. 'The enemy knows we are here now, and they will most likely extinguish the navigation lights after our little session with the patrol-boats.'

The skipper's face tightens, but Tyson is determined to have his say. 'High tide was six hours ago. There will be less than fifty feet of water in the channel. Our two six seven hasn't got the definition at very close range to guide us up through the mudflats, and we will be unable to dive or take evasive action in such a confined area.' He looks at the navigator for confirmation.

Studding smirks. 'That is precisely what everyone will think: including the North Koreans.'

His smile thins. 'I am not so easily put off. We still have several hours of darkness at our disposal, and it looks as though the enemy has given up on us for the time being. As for the navigation, I too have studied the chart, and it shows that we will be pushing into a two knot tide all the way in, but it runs dead in line with our track, so we do not have to worry about drift. A course of zero six zero will get us there without too much bother, and we will have the flow with us when we make our exit. As for the lighthouse: if it is doused we can assume that our two men have run into trouble and the mission is over.'

He hesitates for a moment, looking down at the green baize as though his plans are written there. 'Radar is out. I have no doubt the North Koreans have their own dotted along the shore, and will probably monitor any signals from our own two six seven. Therefore, I am going to rely on our low profile and trim the boat down until the casing is awash. There is a certain amount of slop about, so we will not be easy to see in the dark.'

Tyson is unimpressed. 'Are you not forgetting something, sir? Surely the two Korean officers will have given up on us by now. They will probably believe that we are half-way back to Japan after what they have seen.'

It is just as if the first lieutenant has not spoken. Studding ignores him completely and goes on in a flat, toneless voice. 'It is coming up towards half past midnight. If we get under way by oh one double oh we should complete the nine miles in one hour, and reach the lighthouse by two oclock. There is plenty of water to the west of the island, so I see no reason why we cannot bottom there while someone goes ashore to look for the two men. We will shut down the diesels a mile or so short of the target and creep in on our motors. If I take *Audacity* close in it should not be too difficult to paddle ashore in the rubber dinghy.'

He straightens up to look from one face to another. 'I have driven the boat hard all the way out from Portsmouth, and some of you have doubted my motives. There is an element in the boat, especially amongst the older hands who served in the war, who refuse to take this thing seriously. I am not going to argue that point now. It is sufficient for me to say that this is an important job and we are going to see it through to the best of our ability. Let's face it, compared to some of the things our people got up to during the war this is small beer.'

He turns to Tyson. 'I have taken note of your advice, but I will tolerate no further argument – is that clear?'

We bury our feelings beneath blank stares, but I know the others are sharing the same doubts as me. Studding is living in a world of his own; brushing aside all the obvious dangers and seeing only what he wants to see. If ever a plan was doomed to fail it is this one, for even if we ignore the natural hazards and venture into an area that seems especially designed to trap submarines, we must consider the fact that the North Koreans are on full alert. They are staring out at shadows with itchy fingers, just waiting for us to show. Until today they most likely put aside any notion of a submarine penetrating so far north, but now it is no longer a myth, for they have seen two of their patrol-boats destroyed. For them the night must be filled with all manner of hostile ghosts.

Tyson feels strongly enough to throw caution aside and make one last effort to convince his captain. 'Sir, with due respect, there are only two channels into Chinnampo, and the one to the east of Seki-To is too close to the mainland for us to use. The enemy knows this, and he will be covering the main channel with everything he has got. That stretch of water is barely a mile wide, and I suggest that even during the war no one would have dreamt of making the attempt in such adverse conditions.'

Studding's eyes turn to ice. 'I have warned you against making unhelpful comments; I will not tell you again.'

He switches his eyes to me. 'Normally I would ask for

volunteers, Grant. However, today I have no choice, for you are the only senior man I can spare. I am not going to give you an order, you understand, but you must see the position I am in.'

A solid lump settles at the bottom of my belly. Some men go right through their careers without ever becoming involved with more than their normal duties. Others, like me, seem destined to land in the shit.

'How close can you take the boat in, sir?'

'Within two cables of the western tip of the island – say four hundred yards.'

Too far to swim. That thought had flashed through my head, for a bobbing head is far less conspicuous than a rubber dinghy. 'I shall need a mate, sir. I cannot manage the dinghy on my own.'

'Have you anyone in mind?'

'Yes, sir: Leading Signalman Thorpe. He can bring one of the small signal-lamps with him. I will need to contact the boat, and he is ideal for the job.'

He purses his lips doubtfully. 'I don't want to lose my signalman.'

Tyson intervenes quickly, and I sense that he reads what is running through my mind. 'Any of the telegraphists can handle this end, sir. Both the navigator and myself are reasonably adept with an Aldis, so there should be no real problem.'

Studding still has doubts, but he is tired of argument. He muses over it for no more than a second or two before agreeing reluctantly. 'All right. Take Thorpe if you really think he is the right man.'

I know what he is thinking. The signalman is still suspect in his eyes. A morose odd-ball who seems totally lacking in spirit as he wanders through the boat with a permanent scowl and a big chip on his shoulder.

I know otherwise. As far as I am concerned he is utterly trustworthy, and I need someone like him beside me when I go. Deep down there is an even more compelling reason for selecting him. In many ways Thorpe portrays the effect Studding's hard-nosed attitude is having on the men. The signalman has never known what it is like to be anywhere but on top of the tree. He has shale-oil running through his veins, and has always been treated with deference by his mates. Now his world is shattered, and he finds it impossible to rise above it, so he needs to know that he is respected and trusted. Tyson has seen it too, and is thinking along the same lines. To some it might seem an unwarranted gamble, for there is no shortage of other men available who are equally dependable; but I have no qualms. I have lived amongst men like Thorpe almost all of my service life. They are like incredibly healthy people who are suddenly taken ill. They find it difficult to accept that they can be anything other than perfect, and cannot cope.

'So be it then,' consents Studding when I persist. 'Tell the second coxswain to root out the dinghy and get yourselves prepared.'

He is about to break up the meeting when Welks blusters in with his face strawberry red as he pants out his message. 'I have to report a malfunction in the snort, sir.'

Studding sighs heavily. 'What now?'

The engineer is a bundle of nerves as he assembles his words. 'We have always had problems with the exhaust valve, sir. Normally we shut down the engines one at a time when we stop snorting to prevent water getting into the cylinders. The grinding and operating gear is not reliable, and will have to be sorted out before we can start the starboard engine.'

'How long will that take?'

Welks is never ready with that sort of answer, so Studding must fidget impatiently while the engineer ponders, and he is almost at bursting point before he gets his reply.

'Two hours if we are lucky, sir.'

'And the port engine is all right?'

'As far as I can tell, sir.' Welks's breathing is strained. His eyes are bulging and he trembles with anxiety as he stiffens himself to deliver another piece of bad news. 'There is another problem, sir.'

It is as though his throat is squeezed tight as he perseveres. 'The mast locking-pin is jammed into place. It – it wasn't my fault,' he adds quickly. 'Someone tried to lower it before the pin was out. I – I believe the rod-gearing is damaged because some damned idiot tried to force it.'

He swallows hard as the energy drains from him. If I didn't know what an incompetent sod he is, or how he connives his way through life by riding on the backs of better men, I could almost feel sorry for the poor old devil as he slumps there with dejection rolling off him. He knows that he has muffed it. Any competent engineer with his wits about him would have anticipated these things, as the electrician did. No amount of bluster is going to see him out of this mess.

'So the mast is locked into position,' declares Studding coldly. 'How, in your expert opinion, will this affect our performance?'

Welks gulps hard. Stumbling over his words as he looks down at his shoes. 'Providing we do not have to carry out drastic manoeuvres or dive too deep, we should be all right, sir. I cannot tell the full extent of the damage without investigating it properly, and I cannot do that unless it is flat calm, for I will have to open up the exhaust muffler tank. It is a dockyard job really.'

Studding stares at him for a long time and Welks wilts under his terrible gaze. 'There will be an enquiry, Mr Welks. You had better think hard and come up with some convincing answers, or your career will come to an abrupt end.'

There is a long drawn-out silence while we wait for a decision. Surely now he must call it off!

'We still have the port diesel and both main motors. I can see no reason for aborting at this stage. It may take a little longer to make the passage in,' and here his voice is heavy with sarcasm, 'but I am sure Mr Welks will surpass himself by draining down the starboard diesel and making it operational in record time: Am I right, Chief?'

'Yes, sir,' agrees Welks almost in a whisper.

'Good. Now what is the situation with the port motor, Number one?'

'It has been checked and found to be okay, sir.'

'Right, then let's stop buggering about and get on with it.'

'Sir!' protests Welks miserably.

Studding's eyes are blazing as he rounds on the unfortunate engineer. 'What now?'

'I – I cannot guarantee that we will be watertight when we dive, sir.'

'Just get out of my way, man.' His voice rises to a shout that must be heard throughout the boat. 'Get aft to your oily grotto where you belong, and I want to hear no more from you until you have that engine ready to run – *is that clear?*'

After the engineer has scuttled away Studding gulps down his rage and turns to us again. 'Half ahead group up, Number One. Make sure everyone knows what he has to do, and let's have some extra weight to trim her down. The gun's crew will close up, but the gun hatch will remain shut. They can use the ready-use locker if they have to open fire. Grant; you will make ready to go ashore.' He breathes heavily as he adds fervently, 'Let there be no more interruptions.'

With the diesels shut down there is a strange, muted quiet throughout the boat as the motors drive us into the channel. Thorpe makes no comment when I tell him of my decision, but there is a gleam of life in his eyes for the first time for many days when he listens to the plan.

It takes a while to assemble what we need, and then it is a case of settling down to wait out the hour and a half it will take to reach our objective. Time to ponder on why I am doing all this, and allow thoughts of Zoe to invade my mind. Her face is vague these days, but I know that doesn't mean anything, for I have found it difficult to keep memories in focus after a while, even faces of those who are closest to me. The ache is still as keen, along with the fear that with each passing day we may be growing further apart.

After the initial jolt of anxiety that came when Studding explained his plan a kind of numbed acceptance has taken over. I can't say that I am looking forward to chasing round a chunk of enemy-held rock in the depth of night, but nor am I suffering any real qualms now that I have my thoughts in order. If I shut my mind to all those abstract dreams of domesticity, and visions of my feet propped up on a hearth, with maybe a couple of kids running about the place, a thrill of excitement wells up inside me that I have not felt for a long time.

It has nothing to do with swashbuckling heroics, and I know Thorpe has no notions of glory either. It is as though we have both had a gutful of the intrigue that has gone on for so long, when everyone seems to be taking a hand in the running of our lives. Here is the chance to be rid of that cloying influence for a while, and become totally absorbed in something that will occupy every faculty and push away the petty, private hang-ups. The adrenalin will flow and we shall be out there on our own in the darkness; living on our wits.

Some would call it escapism. Running away from life's hard facts, and indulging in a dangerous game just for the hell of it. The truth is that in all my life I have never felt so immune to fear. It is as if I have suddenly realised how little there is to be afraid of, and how unimportant all the wheelings and dealings of life can be. There is a sort of cold anger inside me as I wait for the signal to go up top. I am doing this for no one but me, and when I crawl out of that hatch to paddle ashore with Thorpe, neither of us will have anyone but ourselves to worry about; and that is how it should be.

I look at him. His face is hollowed and strange in the yellow glow of the lamps as he sits hunched up on the wooden stool. The fore-ends are festooned with swaying oilskins and other articles of clothing hanging from the deckhead. The oily, cylindrical bodies of four torpedo reloads crowd in from either side, and every inch of space is stuffed with gear. The two doors leading into the tubespace are shut, as is the after bulkhead one, leaving us isolated in this shadowed cavern with its profusion of pipes and valves. Almost every inch of pressure hull is used to house some intricate piece of the complicated equipment required to make this undersea beast work. Metal boxes, pipes, dials, valves; all with a specific function, and all glistening in oily stagnation.

A sudden thought hits me. The years I have spent inside these metallic, cigar-shaped bastards may have dulled my appreciation for what goes on ashore. Most of my adult life has been spent balancing against the roll and pitch of submarines, or tensed up while we swim through the dark galleries of the ocean. Is it possible that in this sheltered world, where we are guarded against the traumas of debts and everyday worries, I am unable to face up to the responsibilities of marriage? I cannot really see Zoe settling into a small two up two down, and washing my socks. So I guess my future will be mapped out and paid for by her family whether I like it or not.

I shrug the thoughts away and concentrate on the present. Whatever happens tonight I will go in with my mind clear, and uncluttered with those alien thoughts. Through no effort of his own Studding has got himself a pair of mindless idiots to carry out his plan, but if he thinks for one minute that we are inspired with patriotic fervour, then he is sadly mistaken. Thorpe and I are out to prove nothing to anyone but ourselves.

The after bulkhead door swings open to admit one of the torpedomen. 'You're wanted on the bridge, Swain. You too, Bunts.'

As we go through the boat we are conscious of pale faces staring out from the messes, and the frosty air bites as we emerge from the upper hatch. It takes a moment to adjust my eyes, and when I do I look out across an ocean that is black and filled with noise. Without the throaty mutter of the diesels to push back the sound it closes in on us as we glide through the empty waste. Looking to port I can see nothing but the occasional vague grey-back as it breaks over a half-submerged sand-spit. While to starboard, if I stare hard into the darkness, I can see jagged pinnacles of land eating into the purple sky.

Pushing forward past the periscopes standard I can see the steady white beacon of the Sister's Island light as it beckons us into enemy territory. Perhaps Studding has it right and the two ROK officers are still waiting there as long as the light continues to shine, but I know that if I was in charge of the local garrison, and had captured two spies who were waiting to be picked up, I would make sure that light stayed lit to lure whoever was coming for them right in to my guns.

'Are you ready to go?' The skipper's voice comes thin out of the dark, and I sense rather than see him leaning over the wind-deflector, peering out into the night.

'Yes, sir.' I keep my voice low, and we talk as though the wind is the enemy, for there is no one else to hear us in that empty blackness.

'Good. I do not want the fore-hatch open for longer than absolutely necessary, so you and Thorpe can remain up here and get used to the dark. Try to familiarise yourselves with the area. That's Seki-To over there to starboard, and that is where we can expect gun emplacements and lookout posts. It's only a mile away, so we are at point-blank range if they decide to open fire on us. So far, however, there's been no sign of activity at all, thank heavens!'

He glances at me. 'You should have blackened your faces, but it's too late now; just try to keep your chins buried inside your collars as much as you can.'

He turns away again. 'The chart shows three to five fathoms right up to the edge of the island, and we still have some tide left. With luck we should clear our seventeen foot draught all right, even if I take her almost to the beach. We'll swing to starboard a bit; into the red sector of the light where there is less chance of being illuminated. In a moment we'll open up the fore-hatch and get the dinghy up on to the casing, so you had better have one final – Christ!'

The large expletive is dragged from him when the light suddenly snuffs out to leave a pool of solid darkness across the bow.

'Stop both!'

The sound of the ocean surging past the hull dies until we are left with the soft slop of water against the bilges. In a moment we are wallowing in a circle of silence, straining our ears as our eyes sweep the black void for the first flash of gunfire.

'Don't forget the two knot tide, sir,' whispers Tyson, as the night stays silent. For the first time I am aware of him crouching over the starboard night-sight. 'We are being pushed towards those shoals on the starboard quarter.'

'Yes, all right, Number One,' growls Studding testily. 'I am well aware of it.'

The seconds tick by and still there is nothing. Not a shadow nor a sound to show that anyone knows we are here. It is a weird, uncanny feeling; as though a thousand eyes are watching us. The cold knifes through my spine as I wait with muscles tensed, gripping my stengun tight against my body.

'How far from the lighthouse would you say we are, Pilot?'

Yet another dark shape moves in the gloom beyond the standards. 'About half a mile, sir. The two six seven would tell us exactly.'

'I will not use radar. Half a mile is near enough. How about it, Grant? Can you paddle half a mile?'

I gulp hard. 'I'm still going then, sir?' The words come out before I have time to think. 'I – I thought you said we would abandon everything if the light went out.'

'There could be a dozen reasons for that. If the enemy really knew we were here they would have blasted us out of the water by now. Are you going or not? I can't wait forever.'

Tyson leaps to my aid. 'Surely there is no point in going now, sir?'

'I don't see why not. I noticed the light was extinguished at precisely three o'clock. My guess is that it probably goes out at this time every night. It is just what we need. Grant and Thorpe will have a much better chance of getting ashore unseen.'

'With due respect, sir, that is such a remote possibility that it's no possibility at all,' objects Tyson. 'It is far more likely that someone has seen something to arouse his suspicion. You said we should withdraw in this circumstance.'

'Not if we got this far,' declares Studding. 'They are on a war footing, I'm surprised the light is kept burning at all. If they are looking for shadows, they will concentrate on the channel. It would be suicide to retrace our passage down there until we are certain it is safe. Far better we lay off here, and I intend to carry on as before.' He leans over the voice-pipe. 'Tell the second coxswain to get the dinghy up top.'

He waits for the order to be repeated and relayed through the boat, then bends to the pipe again. 'Slow ahead – group down!'

As the boat moves slowly ahead he opens the metal door leading out on to the gun-platform. 'Down you go, Grant. I'll take you in for a few yards more. Don't forget to keep a low profile. Good luck, both of you.'

It feels a lot colder down here, close to the sea, with the wind rustling through our clothing. The raft is already inflated and in the water, while a couple of men stand by to help us over the side. A hoarsely whispered command comes from the bridge as the boat loses way again, and we both scramble into the bobbing raft and take up the paddles. The solid shape of Sister's Island looms ahead as we get into some sort of rhythm and move out from the black hull.

We shut our minds to the thresh of *Audacity's* screws as she gathers speed towards the west, and paddle in silence as the craggy cliffs take shape ahead of us. The tiny islet is in two parts, with a spit of sand separating them. It is almost awash, and must dry out only at low tide. That is where we are aiming for; hoping to find a sandy cove where the western ridge rises towards the lighthouse. It is a lonely, remote place that makes the corner into the Ping Yong Inlet. We should be clear of any traffic on this side, but only half a mile away from the main island of Seki-to.

'There!'

Thorpe is pointing ahead to where small waves break gently on an outcrop of jagged rocks. There is a small cove just inside of it, fringed with sea-froth. It is about the size of a cabbage-patch, and we drag the dinghy into a tiny cave under the cliff, before taking a moment to weigh up the situation.

'The navy must have a thing about lighthouses,' snorts Thorpe. 'I took part in two landings on the Casquets during the war.'

I am feeling about the flinty rock, looking for an easy way up. We must be careful amongst the small boulders, for a twisted ankle could wreck everything. I find a gulley with a floor of large pebbles running inland to a sloping buttress. It looks as if there is a natural pathway leading up to the left that will take us right to the top of the cliff, close to the lighthouse.

'The sooner we get on with it the better,' I mutter. 'If we stick to that path we can keep our heads below the ridge all the way up.' I look up at the sky. 'We'll move out as soon as the moon gets clear of the cloud.' We slump down together to wait.

'We are dangerous men, you know, Swain,' he mutters suddenly.

'Oh?'

'You're like me. You don't give a sod for anything, so long as you get off the boat. We have no fear, and that can be dangerous.'

The moon is moving out towards the tattered edges of

cloud. 'You mean we are going to "make to die for a free world!"'

'Eh?'

'Never mind,' I grunt as the moon rides free. 'Come on, let's get up that bloody cliff.'

The path is good and we reach the top in quick time, then crouch low on the spiney scrub. According to Studding the ROK officers were brought out here in a sampan, but no one knows for sure whether they were going to take over the lighthouse. We will have to try there first, and then play it by ear. The skipper has allowed us only half an hour, for he wants a couple of hours of darkness to get the boat out of here.

We creep forward with loose rubble crumbling underfoot to cascade down in noisy showers of hard shingle on to the rocks below. I can make out the loom of two small buildings. One is the lighthouse itself, and it is nothing more than a small, square concrete box with a lantern perched on top, the other is square too, and could contain stores, and the keeper's living quarters.

As we get closer I see a flight of steps cut into the rock on the far side of the headland, leading down to a small landing place. There is no sign of a sampan or any other sort of craft, and no sound other than the noise of the sea and our own breathing. We clutch our stens across our bellies, cocked and ready. The island is bathed in purple light and the small door leading into the living quarters stands slightly ajar. Thorpe keeps guard while I slide along the wall to peer into the door.

'Bloody hell!'

'What's up?' he asks when I stagger back and recoil against the wall.

'Take a look for yourself, but don't spew over me.'

I see him shudder when he sees what is inside. Even in the gloom the two bodies, with their slashed throats and staring eyes, are not easy to look at. We take a grip on ourselves and creep into the small, musky room, with its rank stench of humanity. Two corpses have pumped rich blood all over the place, and one look at the wizened old features of the uppermost body convinces me that these are the keepers, for no ROK officer could be that elderly. I feel my right foot slide in the glutinous mess, and that's more than enough for me.

'Come on!' I snap. 'Let's get the hell out of here and take a look at the lighthouse.'

'I think I've lost interest.'

'Shut up and come on.'

Any enthusiasm we had at the outset has disappeared. If we were trained marines we would know the military method of crossing open enemy terrain, but being mere matelots we make a sprint for the door at a low crouching run.

Whoever designed this did not deem it necessary to build a tower, for it is sited on top of a promontory that allows an unrestricted sweep of the light in all direction. The door is on the landward side, and there are two small windows set too far up for us to peer in from the outside. Three steps lead up to the doorstep, and when I push tentatively at the steel door it moves ponderously inwards. Like the living quarters no light shines from within, but the smells are different. This time it is a mixture of body-odour, stale tobacco, urine, oil and rust. I nod at Thorpe, and once again he takes his protective stance while I lift my boot and kick at the door.

There is only one body this time, and if we were in any doubt about the identity of these blokes it is dispelled by what we see. A pathetic little man, dressed in a loose-fitting smock and blossoming trousers, hangs with one arm crooked over the metal door of a switchbox, with his scrawny, ill-fed body draped untidily over a table hinged to the wall. This time he is reasonably tidy, with one neat hole drilled through the centre of his forehead and a dazed expression on his face.

It requires no Sherlock Holmes to sort this out. This bloke

was on the point of dousing the light when he was lumbered. He must have been a plucky little bastard because he managed to rip out a mess of fuses and wire before he died to ensure that no one lit it up again. I can imagine the mad scamper as they tried to reach him before he could throw the switch, but he was too quick for them.'

'The sods!' croaks Thorpe with a catch in his voice. 'They did all this and then scarpered.'

I nod. 'My guess is that they held these keepers hostage until pick-up time, and when they saw the fireworks and we didn't turn up at the allotted time, they decided to do away with this lot and try to make it overland. This poor sod was more than they bargained for. He hoped that if he doused the lamp the authorities would realise that something was wrong, and send out a boat to investigate. Right now I'd say that *Audacity* could be in danger. It depends on what the Commies have in the way of anti-submarine vessels, and how quick they react to the situation.'

'It is time I got to work with my little old lamp then.'

'Yes. You'd better call up the boat and spell out the bad news, then we can get down to the dinghy and paddle like hell.'

He thinks for a moment as he looks about the small compartment. There is a steel ladder leading up through the roof on to the lantern platform, but the old Korean's legs are draped across it. Thorpe goes across and takes hold of the body. It lifts away so easily it takes him off guard.

'He's a skinny old bastard,' grunts the signalman as he drags the body towards me and stretches it out on the deck. 'Must have eaten about once a month I reckon. Hold 'im up to the light and you could see right through.'

'You want to go up top?' I ask.

'We'll have all round vision up there,' he explains as he makes his way to the foot of the ladder. 'You can look round while I call up the boat.'

'All right,' I agree. 'Get up top, and let's hope they are keeping a good lookout.'

There is a metal plinth running round the base of the lantern house about thigh-high, while the upper part is like an elaborate conservatory, with glass panels set in a metal frame. In the centre sits the lamp itself, and even in the deep gloom there is a hint of red in its achromatic lenses.

When I look east I see twinkling white lights spangled in ones and twos along the coast, with small clusters strung out in groups here and there on Seki-To. Further away two flashing lights mark the entrance to the inlet: one red, one white. They are about seven miles away, and my guess is that trouble will come from Seki-To, or a patrol-boat if they have any left. There is no immediate danger, and I find myself thinking calm and clear, with my old confidence flooding back again. Behind me I can hear Thorpe preparing to make his signal, and I am about to look back towards him when I notice something between the two flashing lights.

'Hold it, Bunts!' I warn urgently. 'There's a ship out there. I saw it move across the shore lights a moment ago. Look, there it is again!'

A low black shape is moving towards us, and I make my mind up quickly. 'Get your bloody lamp working!'

'Won't they see the lamp?' he asks.

'No. I don't think so. They are coming straight for us and the island is between them and the submarine. Anyway, we've got no choice. If we don't warn Studding the boat will be at risk.'

'I'll make it brief then.' He kneels down behind the plinth to rest the lamp on its rim. *Audacity* must be on full alert, for the answering flicker comes immediately. Thorpe spells out the words slowly; dictating to me as he goes. *'Keeper's dead – Enemy patrol-boat heading this way – We are alone.'*

The submarine's lamp blinks an acknowledgement, then all goes dark while we wait for Studding to make up his mind what to do next. I get a horrible feeling that we are really on our own now. There is no time to get down to the dinghy and paddle out to *Audacity* before that boat reaches the island. If she is to get down through the passage and well clear before daylight she must go now. She might take on the patrol-boat, but the shore batteries will surely sink her if she tries to run the gauntlet, and with the snort out of commission she would have to run out on the surface to make up time and get through before dawn breaks. It's no use trying to squat on the bottom to wait for a more opportune moment either, for they would find her easily in that restricted area.

Her aldis starts to blink again. '*Sorry – Must leave you – Hold on for daylight – Will send help – Good luck.*'

Thorpe triggers a reply, then sets about arranging his three spare magazines in a neat row beside him. 'How long before daybreak,' he asks laconically.

'About an hour.'

'And how long before that gook boat gets here?'

'About twenty minutes at a rough guess.'

'Think we can hold out?'

'Not if she starts lobbing shells at us.'

He ponders for a moment. 'Maybe they won't want to wreck the lamp.'

'Maybe,' I grunt.

'Do you reckon they'll take us prisoner?'

I look at him. 'If you saw what's been done to the keepers would you take us prisoner?'

'Not bloody likely!'

'Well then, don't ask stupid questions.'

I try to imagine what Studding has in mind as I check the magazines. What was it that Marine sergeant used to bawl at us so long ago in Malta? 'Aim low. Use short bursts, and keep the enemy's head down. Don't expect to hit anything; you lot would be more dangerous throwing snowballs.'

'You take this side, Bunts. I'll squat here. Try not to show yourself, but keep them outside grenade-throwing range if possible, or we'll end up splattered all over the glasswork.'

'I know one sod I'd like to shoot,' he glurts out grimly.

'Oh?'

He pauses for a second, as though making up his mind if

he should say any more, then it all comes flooding out. 'In case anything goes wrong, Swain. There's something you should know.'

'What?'

'It's about Welks and Subby.'

'What about them?' I am watching the oncoming boat. It is moving more slowly than I thought. 'Can't it wait?'

He ignores me. 'Welks was ridin' Subby's back. He found out that Subby was more keen on boys than girls and never let him forget it.'

I can see the outline of the boat now. It looks like a harbour tug, pushing up a huge bow-wave with her blunt stem. 'Why go into it now, for Christ's sake!' I snarl at him. 'why not let it rest, and allow the poor sod to keep his secret?'

'Because it was Mr Bloody Welks who messed about with the distiller and the air-conditioner, that's why. He's bin doing all he can to delay us. Even trying to arrange a court martial for yours truly.'

'Why?'

He grins bitterly. 'Didn't you see how he shook when he was telling the skipper about the snort? He wasn't far off spewin' his guts up. He is a gutless bastard, Swain. Shit-scared of comin' to Korea.'

'How'd you find out?'

'Subby told me. A couple of days out from Singapore one of Welks's young stokers came to him with the stolen gear and admitted pinching it and then tryin' to make it look like I'd done it. It was bloody sick, Swain. He was cryin' when he told me that he'd gone straight to Welks with it, and the bastard had turned on him and threatened to shop him if he breathed a word to anyone.'

'What did you say?'

'I told him to tell you or Tyson.'

'And?'

'He said he couldn't face up to it, but if I wished I could shop the bloody lot of them myself.' He hesitates for a moment as though he finds the memory hurtful. 'I told him to do his own dirty work, but he didn't have the guts. I reckon he just did the next best thing and plonked the gear on the wardroom table to get me off the hook.'

'You were wrong to keep it to yourself. Welks could endanger the boat.'

He snorts derisively. 'Not him. He won't do anythin' to risk his own neck. It wouldn't surprise me if that snort hasn't made a miraculous recovery.'

We go silent and concentrate on the approaching boat as it swings out in a wide arc to head in towards the landing. Three or four minutes and they will be here. 'What wouldn't I give for a rifle,' I mutter, tapping the cold metal of my sten. 'These bloody things are useless until they are almost on top of us.'

'Perhaps we'd do better down amongst the rocks,' he suggest as he points towards the bluff that overlooks the landing.

I shake my head. 'Wherever we go they'll have the edge on us. At least from here we have got all-round vision and a certain amount of cover. If we keep low the rim of the concrete wall will stop anything smaller than a shell, and the plinth keeps us hidden. We must try and pick them off as they climb the steps.'

'Then what?'

'Hold out till dawn and trust that Studding knows what he's talking about. The sun should be coming up in forty minutes or so. I think it's getting lighter even now.'

'Studding can't perform miracles,' he comments morosely.

'It'll be okay,' I reassure him. 'Now shut up – they're here!'

The tug is sliding in slowly. Rolling in the backwash from the cliffs as it noses in cautiously. As far as I can see she has no large gun, but there are a couple of twin-mounted machine-guns each side of her bridge, and huddled shapes of soldiers lining her bulwarks. At a rough estimate I'd say about thirty men in all.

The landing was built for small boats, and the tug skipper

is having his work cut out to bring her in without running her bows on to the rocks or ramming the jetty. Twice, just as it looks like he is going to make it, he goes full astern and backs out for another go. I can hear argument and shouting, as though someone is tearing him off a strip for being so cagey. I bless his incompetence, for every second he farts about is like gold to us.

Now she comes in more determinedly. It looks like someone with more bottle has taken over. She is blustering in at a speed that must ram her bow firmly into the small cove alongside the jetty. Her captain must be wringing his hands, for she could rip out her side if she strikes it badly. We hear the screech of tortured metal as she hurtles into the landing. Already the mustard-coloured uniformed pongoes are leaping over the gun'ls, and moving with monkeylike agility as they mount the steps.

Forgetting all we've been taught about conserving ammo we open fire in a concerted, concentrated burst, and the leading shapes scatter or fall back amid a chorus of shouts and screams. I remove my empty magazine and clip another in place shamefully. The enemy has melted into the scenery, or leapt back into the relative shelter of the tug's bulwark. Half a dozen shots come from somewhere, whanging like angry bees through the metalwork above our heads.

'Just one grenade is all I need to splatter that lot,' growls Thorpe wishfully.

'You'd have to get close enough first,' I grunt soberly. 'Keep your head down and your bursts short. We are gonna need every round.'

IX

'It's definitely getting lighter,' mutters Thorpe hopefully.

I can see that the deep purple is turning a shade brighter, and that the sky is becoming gun-metal blue, with a sliver of yellow showing above Seki-To. From somewhere below us comes a prolonged scream, and I glance at my watch. Seven minutes have gone by since the tug made its first approach.

Another shot ricochets past my left ear, and I loose off another couple of bursts. Controlled this time; no more than four or five rounds at a squeeze. So far so good. All they can do is crouch low and take pot shots at us. Already the dawn is showing; though what help that can bring is lost to me. *Audacity* is probably churning south towards the Yellow Sea, and the nearest Allied ship is about one hundred and fifty miles away.

Suddenly the heavy stutter of machine-guns opens up and we both cringe as a fusillade of shots smash through the glass and steel framework, sending showers of debris raining down. All we can do is flatten ourselves into the concrete and pray as the atmosphere above us is ripped apart. The metal plinth is turning into a colander as bullets zing through it as though it was made of cheese. I shut my eyes and try to dissolve into the deck.

Eventually I force them open again to look for more substantial cover. Ten feet to my right an upright stanchion takes the weight of the lamp's canopy, and looks solid enough to hide a man and keep him reasonably safe if he tucks himself well in. I roll over towards it, trying to ignore the tracer lancing through the air inches above me. I catch a couple of breaths and ease myself into the corner as I straighten up carefully to bring my eye level with a small aperture where the screen joins the strut. From here I can peer out without showing myself.

They haven't lost much time. The leading men are already clear of the steps and spreading out in crouching runs to take up positions amongst the scree and scattered boulders. I fire a quick burst at them and send them diving into the ground, then realise with horror that I have left behind my spare magazines.

'Bunts!' I call for a whispered shout at the figure still sprawled behind the plinth, and for a moment he looks dead. Then his face turns towards me.

'Try and get to the other corner strut, and don't forget your ammunition.'

Now I know he was the right choice, for he wriggles towards me, and with a couple of quick movements, sends my magazines skating across the smooth concrete. I grab them eagerly and turn back to the job. The Koreans have recovered and are busy deploying themselves for an attack. They flitter from boulder to boulder, and I can hear shouts as they take up position for the final assault.

Both heavy machine-guns keep up their steady chatter from the tug, and when I look along the plinth to where Thorpe is pulling himself into his corner there is not an inch of it that is not perforated with bullet holes.

I am getting selective now. Firing short bursts at real targets, and my head is remarkably cool. I am surprising myself today, for apart from a few isolated moments of panic I have no fear. It is as though I no longer care what happens to me, just as Thorpe said. I have no feelings for those animated wretches dashing about below; just a cold, calculating need to kill them before they reach the tower. I know my firing gives away my position, and I cringe back instinctively when a hail of fire snarls past my ears, but I am ready when one stupid sod tries to make an heroic dash for the door. He performs a perfect somersault when my bullets smash into his body.

The door is situated so that anyone who tries to reach it must come under a cross-fire from Thorpe and myself now that he's in position, and we do not need to expose ourselves while we pick them off. Not that it offers much solace, for I know damned well that although we can pick them off while they keep making these abortive attempts to rush the tower, all they really need to do is wait for us to run out of ammo, or creep in close enough to lob a couple of hand-grenades through the broken windows.

As if they have read my thoughts a heavy object clunks against the plinth, and bounces back to explode with a loud bang on the ground below. It deafens me for a second, and I shake my head to clear my brain. It seems to restore my sanity, for I suddenly remember that I have not only myself to think about. I am supposed to be in command, and it is up to me to decide when the situation is hopeless enough to try and save ourselves by surrendering. Maybe they won't just hang us up by the balls.

Another grenade spins off the concrete and pounds into my brain, forcing me to concentrate my thoughts. Another hail of fire snarls past my head, and another suicidal figure makes a wild dash for the door, to run into a concerted barrage that changes his zig-zagging run into a macabre jig before he hits the deck.

The bedlam is ceaseless. The sharp staccato of automatics and the heavier rhythm of the MGs from the tug, punctuated now and again by the reverberating bangs of exploding grenades. Above our heads pieces of lighthouse splinter and crash, adding its contribution to the madness. I see no future in this. The moment has surely come when I must do something to try and save our skins; but how do I surrender? I doubt if there is anyone amongst that angry mob who is the slightest bit interested in Geneva Conventions. In my pocket I have a white handkerchief, and I could try sticking my hand out to wave it at them, but when I look at the sieve that was once a solid metal plinth the idea dissolves at once. The only answer is to yell out at the top of my voice and hope that someone understands English.

I see Thorpe glaring at me. His pale face is blank in the bleak light of a growing dawn. I give him a 'thumbs down,' and he nods back. We shrink into our corners and wait for the next lull in the firing, or at least a lessening in its intensity. I draw a deep breath and prepare to shout, 'I surrender!' hoping that it is the one phrase that has been taught to their officers.

The screaming howl of diving aircraft swamps all other sound, and I look up to see the big engine cowl of a Sea Fury aimed straight at me. Two streaks of fire and smoke arc out from beneath its wings straight for the hiding places of the troops below, and I follow their trajectory right into the ground, and hear the screams of wounded men after the explosions. There are white United Nations stripes on their wings as the aircraft pulls out to soar up in climbing turns to make room for their mates.

They must come from *Neptune,* and they must have taken off before dawn to reach us now. The first four carry out the rocket attacks with a precison that warms my blood, but I notice that they are concentrating on the island, even though the tug must present a fine target as it sits beside the jetty with its MGs firing ineffectively into the sky. I see a formation of Four Fireflys peeling off to make bombing runs with anti-personnel bombs. All Thorpe and I can do is squat down and cover our heads while the atrocious sound takes over.

The first four Furys have made their turns, formed up, and are coming in again with their cannons pounding away. I turn to Thorpe in time to see the idiot break cover to leap about waving at the pilots like a madman.

'Keep down, you oaf!' I scream at him as he prances about like a maniac, and he sobers up to look at me with a startled expression, before flinging himself down and scrambling on all fours towards his strut. He hasn't gone a yard before he yells out and sprawls out flat, with his legs jerking, and rolling in agony amongst the debris.

Another shadow swoops across, and I look up to see a Firefly banking into a tight turn with the observer's canopy pulled right back so that he can wave at me with both hands above his head. I haul myself fully upright to wave back, forgetting all I told Thorpe about keeping his head down. I must make a strange sight as I stand there amongst the debris with my sten gun hanging loose in my hand, and Thorpe lying propped up against my legs. High above us four Sea Furys form up to head back south, while a new formation arrives to take their place. I scan the opaque surface of the sea, half expecting to see a destroyer churning up out of the haze that sits like a shroud across the horizon. The day has taken on a sultry aspect as the watery sun rises clear of Seki-To: An oriental seascape with scattered junks sitting like frozen statues with their sails hanging limp in the dead air. Only the continuous howl of flying war machines destroys the ethereal beauty of it, for the firing has died to a few sporadic bursts.

Lifting my eyes I see yet another pair of fighters coming in, and when I drop my gaze I see that they are escorting another shape that skims the surface and takes a long time to materialise into the old-fashioned outlines of a throwback from another era: a relic from a bygone war with twin wings and a radial engine above the fuselage. The Sea Otter makes even the junks look up to date as it makes its slow, sedate approach while shore batteries take pot shots at it. Like other enemy gunners who have come to grips with ancient aircraft like Swordfish and Otters there is confusion amongst the layers who refuse to accept that any modern machine can be so pedestrian. Their 'aim-off' is all to cock, so their shells tend to pass ahead or astern of the target as it drones by at the speed of a fast car.

A soft groan draws my attention away from the flying circus. 'You okay?' I ask as I bend to take a look at the recumbent signalman.

'Am I buggery!' He gasps, rolling over on to his side and clasping a hand to his rump. 'They've shot me in the arse.'

'Well stay low, for Christ's sake!' I warn as the howl of another Firefly shatters the sky and its dark shape swoops over us.

'As if I had a choice,' he complains.

'Where does it hurt?'

He takes a moment to prod about. 'It's just a sort of dull ache at the base of my spine. My brain is telling my feet to move, but they won't operate.' He shudders. 'I feel lousy.'

'Try to lie still while I take a look.'

'Don't get any ideas.'

I have to grin. It has taken all this to restore his humour. 'I've got no desire to examine your buttocks, me old son. I want to see if there's a chance of us getting out of here.'

The shooting has really stopped now as I crawl up to the plinth and lift my head to peer over the top. It is like looking at the moon. The whole area is smoking, pock-marked wilderness, with the acrid stench of burnt explosives wafting up to me; along with subdued groans of wounded men. A few healthy tail-enders are scampering for their lives down the steps and into the tug, which shows every sign of pulling out without them. Some of the more conscientious are helping injured mates along, but most have only one thing in mind – a healthy future.

There is a last minute scramble when they realise the tug is on the move, and the survivors start yelling frantically and abandoning their protesting burdens as they see salvation slipping away. Anyone who is not fully mobile is dumped as everyone fends for himself in the final avalanche of humanity that tumbles down the steps. With the screech of tortured metal the tug wrenches herself off the shingle and drags her crumpled bow into deep water.

The sadistic aircraft wait until the tug is well away from the shore with its leaky bow-down angle and cringing cargo before they come in with precise, copy-book attacks. The antiquated craft doesn't stand a chance as the rockets find their target. It stops and swings sideways out of control with flames and smoke pouring from the upper-deck. Figures are leaping over the side, and within a short time there is nothing left but a swirl of wreckage and bobbing heads.

Turning back to Thorpe I find him lying face up and looking like death. 'It's now or never, mate,' I urge him gently, and he gives a weak smile. 'I'll make you as comfortable as I can, so try and bear with me.'

I use my own webbing to truss up his legs, and all the time he looks at me as though he isn't sure what's going on. Just as well, for I suspect that if he had any feelings at all I couldn't bear to hear his screams. As it is I am sure there is an accusing look in his eyes, and it is hard to say whether he knows anything of what is happening to him.

I have left his webbing on, for it makes a sort of harness that I use to drag him across to the ladder and lower him down as gently as possible.

I cannot believe that I am not causing pain as I ease him down and prop him against the wall, yet he makes no sound other than his strangled breathing and an occasional grunt. He looks ghastly, and in other circumstances I wouldn't move him another inch, but I can imagine the kind of treatment he will receive if I leave him to the mercy of the Koreans when they take stock of the carnage.

Once he is settled I go to the door and look out at the smoking scrubland. I can see several bodies scattered in untidy heaps amongst the rocks, and they are half hidden by a ground-mist that swallows my legs when I make a dash for the nearest boulder. I crouch and listen for signs of life amongst the dead and injured, then, when I am sure there are no avenging bastards lying in wait, I head back to the door.

With great difficulty I manage to hoist him over one shoulder and stagger to the door. The landscape stays quiet as I shrug his weight into a more comfortable position and receive a grunt for my efforts. 'Sorry, Bunts,' I pant. 'I've got no time for finesse. I'll do it as quickly as possible.'

It is like carrying a sack of spuds, and the hand I use to grip his thigh is becoming saturated with blood. I wade through the mist, watching and listening for signs of life amongst the bodies. There is movement and human noises, but nothing threatening. I reach the top of the natural ramp that leads down to the base of the cliff, and start slipping and sliding on the loose rubble, trying to keep my footing, and almost breaking into a gallop as the slope increases. Finally we fall in an untidy mess on to the beach.

It takes only a few seconds to haul the dinghy from its hiding place and launch it. The hard part is lifting Thorpe on board, for he is unconscious now, and his limbs flop all over the place. I have to stand waist-deep in the icy water while I work his limp torso aboard. The soft ripple of wavelets wash in from the placid sea, bobbing the dinghy about to increase my problems, but eventually I am able to hoist myself up beside him with a series of undignified jerks.

It is awkward trying to paddle on my own, and I work the dinghy out in an ungainly, revolving zig-zag, until a helpful little current takes hold and pushes me clear of the clawing attraction of the shore.

The antiquated grumble of the Sea Otter's Bristol Mercury grows as she circles to make an exploratory run past the dinghy, scouring the surface for obstacles before committing herself to a landing. I wave both hands at the pale faces staring out at me as they go by. One helmeted figure is standing with his head and shoulders sticking out of the roof, dangerously close to the whirring propeller. She looks like a pre-historic bird as she lumbers into a tight bank.

Now she turns into her final approach with one wing-tip almost brushing the surface. I have always had a fascination for seaplanes and flying boats, and I have watched big Sunderlands touch down in Sasebo harbour with hardly a ripple. The tips of their hulls skimming the water with barely a blemish, before gradually settling with great dignity. I wince as the Otter plunges into the drink like an old sea-boot, to come waddling up in a welter of spray and foam with about as much grace as a distraught pelican.

The observer's helmet comes within inches of being sliced

off as he climbs out of the cockpit and on to the prow, clutching a coiled-up heaving-line in one hand, and desperately clinging to his perch with the other, as this updated version of the old Walrus wallows towards me. I can see now why those old war-horses had the propeller mounted at the rear of the engine, and I wonder what sadistic bastard decided to put it on the front so that it can decapitate unsuspecting people who are careless about the way they emerge from the hatch on the roof.

I stop paddling and allow the Otter to splash up to us with a great amount of roaring and spluttering, until the heaving-line snakes out to land across the dinghy. Full marks to the bloke on the bow, for he has to use one hand for his own safety all the time, and the plane is bobbing about in the wash she stirred up when she made her ungainly landing.

Much of the hauling is left to me, for all he can do is hang on tightly to his end and take the strain. There is a handy little rail attached to the hull, specially designed for these occasions, and placed to provide hand or footholds for unfortunate sods like me who are subjected to the dubious pleasure of being rescued from a watery grave.

The bloke in the helmet has no time for niceties as he reaches down to grab a fistful of Thorpe's clothing when I hoist his shoulders up. With me pushing from behind the signalman goes up like a bag of last week's washing on to the bow, and I'm left to struggle on my own until all three of us are on the snub nose.

The blades of the propeller are just ticking over as I help the airman to lift Thorpe up to the windscreen. Calvin is in the left seat staring out at me with an expression that is about as welcoming as a wet sock. He wears a service cap with earphones clamped over it, and a Mae West over his uniform. The ubiquitous observer has not uttered one word throughout, but as I gather strength to hoist the signalman up over the top and into the hatch he stops and peers hard into Thorpe's face.

'I think your mate is dead, chief,' he yells above the noise of the engine.

'No, he isn't,' I declare forcefully. 'Let's get him inboard.'

He studies my face and decides it isn't worth arguing. Together we hump Thorpe down into the sanctuary of the cabin and stretch him out on the deck. It is cramped and spartan in here, and I find myself pushed into a canvas seat and offered a flying helmet and Mae West. The cold is getting to work on me and sapping away my energy. All I can do is meekly submit while he plugs in the 'jack' for the earphones. Some unintelligible garbage rattles in my ears and he is shaking my shoulders as though he is trying to force life back into me.

'You press this button if you wish to speak,' he shouts. 'Try not to fall asleep.'

I nod obedience, hoping he will go away and leave me in peace with Thorpe, but he breaks out a flask from somewhere and floods my mouth with hot liquid. I choke for a moment, then it sears my gullet and lifts me out of my apathy a bit, so I take a longer swig and relish its warmth. He tucks a blanket round my shoulders before going forward to his seat.

'Hold tight!'

Calvin sounds like a bus conductor, and the engine explodes with a bellowing roar as the hull judders and begins to surge forward. That drink must have been laced for I can still feel its glow, and my senses are holding firm enough to take stock of what is going on. We are ploughing along with spray showering the windows, and I can feel her buffeting against the slop. The howl of the engine lifts to an impossible crescendo, threatening to tear her apart as she struggles to break free of the cloying embrace of the sea. We hit a couple of ridges, bounce into the sky, hang there for a moment, then skip a wave or two before soaring up into a banking climb.

I am recovered enough to think about Thorpe, and I lean over his outstretched torso to pull down the blanket from his face. A thick lump clogs my throat when I see his ashen face. I have never seen anyone look more dead, and there is no sign of breathing as he lies there with his eyes firmly shut. The Otter is jumping about, for Calvin is almost wave-hopping, but I release my safety belt and kneel down beside Thorpe to listen for a sound of breathing. It's a useless exercise, for the noise of the engine drowns all else. I place a couple of fingers on his neck where I imagine his pulse to be, and find nothing. Not that it means much, because I could be inches away from the right spot. I ease back into my seat, still staring at his quiet face, unwilling to accept that he is gone.

The Otter drones on. I am too exhausted and cold to do more than sit with my thoughts. They refuse to form a pattern and I am left with a jumble of dissociated ideas that play on the edge of sleep. If I look out of the window I see a plain of glistening silver, and I am mesmerised by its monotony.

I must have slept for some time, because when I wake I find the observer shaking my shoulders and admonishing me. 'I told you not to sleep,' he complains. 'Come on, we're almost home.'

I protest weakly, but he is an insistent bastard. He heaves me upright and points towards the windscreen. 'Look, there's the carrier!'

Forcing my brain to function I blink across Calvin's shoulder at the olive sea and the dark shapes of ships.

'That's *Neptune* to starboard!' he yells eagerly. 'And that's a Yankee carrier over to port. She's our relief.' He fiddles with my safety belt and takes it in a notch or two. 'You ever landed on a carrier?'

I shake my head. Even that awesome prospect fails to excite me. I watch her absentmindedly as we make a pass down her starboard side, crossing over her attendant destroyer as we go. The sea-boat's crew will be manning the whaler in case Calvin makes a cock of things. *Neptune* looks smaller than I remember; but that could be psychological.

The rum and the exhaustion have dulled my senses and left me unconcerned, but I'm still able to pray that Calvin controls the Otter better than his horse.

The horizon disappears as we bank into the final approach with hook and wheels lowered. I can see a bloke standing splaylegged waving table tennis bats at us, and we seem to be creeping up on her as though there is a chance we may not catch up with her twenty knots. Eventually, however, we plop down with the grace of a farmyard hen.

Blokes wearing coloured, tight-fitting helmets and waist-coats dash out to wave more tennis bats at us. Calvin opens the throttle and we trundle forward across the collapsed crash-barriers and on to the forward lift. A bell tolls a monotonous dirge as the sky disappears and we drop down into the hangar. It looks like they want to get this relic out of sight before the Yanks on the other carrier do themselves injury when they fall about laughing.

It is deathly quiet now that the engine is stopped and the bell silenced. We are being towed astern with the wings folded, and parked in what looks like a large factory, full of aircraft with naked engines and gaping fuselage. The Otter is pushed into a corner, and men with red crosses lift Thorpe out of the cabin, then help me to climb down on to the deck. They hold me upright all the way to the sickbay, strip off my clothes and dump me into a snug cot. I hardly have time to blink before the lights go out.

Twenty-four hours later I am in the chiefs' mess listening to them bragging about the way they operate. There is a pride amongst them when they explain how they get more aircraft into the air in shorter time than the Yanks, despite the fact that they have only one catapult to her two. They have brought their recovery rate down to below fifteen seconds per aircraft. Drill drill drill, that's what it takes, and their record for safe landings stands at over a thousand without so much as a burst tyre. No small feat when the Firefly has a reputation for being a 'bouncer' with a belly-hook that tries to ignore arrester wires.

They are full of themselves, and justifiably so by my reckoning. It is something we seem to have lost in *Audacity*. Something fresh and infectious that should be there, but isn't. Yet no one is more drill-conscious than Studding, so where did we go wrong? Looking at these lively faces gives me an answer. There is a heart in this crew: a genuine eagerness to perform well for their own pride, and not just because one man considers he deserves their excellence as a matter of course, without putting anything back.

The chief sitting next to me while I eat my meal is at pains to make me understand why conserving aircraft is so important. 'It isn't just swank, Chief. Our replacement aircraft have to be brought all the way from Singapore on the old *Unicorn*. We are on our way to meet her in Kure now. She will transfer a new quota and take off the ones we cannot service ourselves. Every plane is precious: too precious to throw away on bad landings or bad drill.'

'How long is a stint?' I ask, not the least bit put off by their bragging, for it is done in no self-congratulatory way. They have a professional standard to live up to, and a pride in the way they have proved themselves under wartime conditions.

'It takes three days to travel to and from out billet off the west coast. We spend the first four days up there flying as many as two hundred sorties, and we are getting better all the time,' he says with a huge grin on his chubby face. 'After four days we withdraw to a safe area and meet up with a Royal Fleet Auxiliary tanker to refuel and store up, then it is another four days of intensive flying before the Yanks come up to relieve us.

'Each carrier is supposed to do a six month tour. It is not World War Two stuff by any means, and only the aircrews get to see the real fighting. All we get is a lot of hard work and "four hours on – four hours off – defence stations" for most of the time. We've had a couple of sub scares that turned into shoals of fish, and our radar boys picked up a contact closing at five hundred knots which developed into a friendly destroyer bringing up the mail. Apart from that, and some "mines" that became jellyfish, it has been a quiet life.'

*

Sailing across the Inland Sea into Kure is like riding through a huge lake, with ferries crossing our path as we make stately progress towards the big naval dockyards. There are numerous fishing boats and islands dotted about with shrines growing out of the top, making it all look like something out of *The Mikado*. Eventually we berth alongside a jetty dominated by a huge crane, used to transfer the aircraft between the two carriers. According to the chubby-faced chief the jetty is an upturned battleship with a kind of drawbridge connecting it to the shore.

Unicorn is a real workhorse, looking a bit bigger than her sixteen and a half thousand tons, with her high freeboard and ungainly lines. She is an unsung heroine, carrying out her mundane duties ranging from the ferrying of Japanese ex-prisoners of war and squaddies, to bringing up replacement stores and aircraft for the operational carriers. The whole set-up is cold and businesslike, with no flag-waving or glory-seeking overtones. Both ships are here to do a job, and they get on with it as quietly and efficiently as they can.

As soon as we are tied up I am ordered to report to Lieutenant-Commander Longman in *Unicorn's* ship's office. He turns out to be a friendly, unassuming man who makes me feel at ease immediately.

'I have been instructed to arrange transfer for you to return to the UK, Grant. You will be issued with a uniform and the remainder of your gear sent on from *Audacity*.'

'Where is she, sir?'

'Half way to Hong Kong by now, I should think. She is being held over for some sort of enquiry before she rejoins the Fleet.'

The temptation to say nothing and just get on that plane back home is great, yet I cannot leave it like that. 'I am surprised I haven't been summoned to take part in that enquiry, sir.'

'Oh?'

I explain about Subby, but leave out Thorpe's disclosures, and when I'm done he shrugs and smiles. 'I can understand your concern, but I cannot see that your presence will make any change to the outcome. I would take advantage of what's on offer if I were you.'

'That's what you think!' my mind tells him, but I keep my mouth firmly shut. Maybe it is about time I began to think of myself. After all, what would I achieve if I did spill the truth? Nothing but to stir up a lot of dirt, and much of it would stick to Subby. After the way Welks behaved off Korea his service career is on the skids anyway. So, there is nothing to be gained in sticking my neck out.

'Thank you, sir. That is what I would like to do.'

'Good!' He breathes a sigh of relief and shuffles some papers about. 'I think I have everything here, but your flight is not until the day after tomorrow, so you can live in *Unicorn* for now.' He smiles widely. 'Perhaps you would like to visit your friend in hospital.'

'Sorry, sir?'

He frowns. 'Your companion. He is recovering in hospital, only a few steps outside the dockyard gate.'

I can't accept what I am hearing. 'Are you talking about Leading Signalman Thorpe, sir?'

'Who else?' He sees the look in my face. 'Is something wrong?'

I gulp hard. 'I thought he was dead, sir.'

He relaxes again. 'Good heavens no! I am glad to tell you that he is very much alive. If you wish I can arrange for a jeep to take you to him.'

'That I would like, sir.'

The hospital is only five minutes away. A huge building standing beside the road with a flood-ditch in front of it and a drawbridge to the door. Thorpe is in a room on his own and looks out of his element in the antiseptic atmosphere. There is a rubber hose running under the bedclothes from a blood bottle, and his face is white. When he sees me he grins, and for a moment we stare at each other like a couple of idiots.

'I thought you were dead, you old sod!'

A slight cloud crosses his features, but he grins back. 'Not quite, Swain – not quite.'

Something in his tone wipes the smile from my face. 'When are you gonna be up and about again?'

It is the wrong question, and I should have known better than to ask it. He still smiles, but it is different now, and it doesn't show in his eyes. 'There's only half of me still working,' he says with an ache in his voice. 'No more dirty runs ashore or anything that requires movement below the belt.'

After that our conversation is false. We both hide the truth under a barrage of flippant words and welcome the time when a nurse comes to say that I must go. Outside the cold sunshine emphasizes the drabness of the dockyard. There is a canteen filled with Australians knocking back booze as fast as they can while they stand in a pool of spilt beer. The noise is tremendous, and a gaggle of pongoes is cheering on some idiot who is trying to eat a tumbler. I swallow my half pint and leave with a new anger welling inside me. I am on my way to find Longman and tell him how I have changed my mind, and how important my evidence is for the enquiry.

He is reluctant at first, but there is no arguing with someone who is willing to throw aside his future to make sure the truth is told. Whether I attend the hearing or not people are going to learn about Welks.

I travel in a Dakota with a motley crowd of personnel from all nations and services, and I stay silent for all of the way until we touch down at Kai Tak. They gave me a replacement uniform, but I have sweated enough to make it soggy and shapeless by the time I leap down from the tailboard of the three-tonner on to the old familiar jetty where the hut with the grid over its window stares out of the gloom to remind me of dangling shoes and boggling eyeballs.

Tyson and Solomon are supervising the loading of stores when I arrive, and they welcome me with broad grins and a smattering of friendly banter as I bounce across the plank. I walk through the boat, exchanging greetings with several of the crew until I reach the chiefs' mess, where I shed my stale clobber, wrap a towel round my waist and commandeer the only shower for the time it takes to wash away the accumulated filth from my body.

Afterwards, freshly shaved, clothed and groomed, I feel fit enough to face Studding when he calls me to the wardroom. Tyson has left his work to join in the interview, and I must be well in favour for I am offered a whisky before they begin asking questions.

I don't need much egging on, and once I am in full flow they remain silent all the way through. I leave out all the personal bits and pieces and stick to the facts as I talk in a flat, toneless voice. I make no mention of Thorpe's disclosures, for I want that to come at the right time, so that I can savour the look on Welks's face and relish his condemnation when everyone learns the truth.

Studding waits until he is sure I have finished before he speaks. 'You are to receive a special mention for your efforts at Chinnampo, Grant, and I am delighted to bring you more practical news. You are to be offered the rank of lieutenant. It is a specialist appointment, so you won't even have to go through the normal exams and such. Just as if you were a doctor or a schoolmaster in fact. I'm sure you know the drill. Only in your case you have done an awful lot to earn it, and in the process brought credit to all of us in *Audacity*. Allow me to be the first to congratulate you.'

He holds out his hand and I accept it automatically. To become a two-ringer overnight is hard to come to terms with after all that's gone on, especially for a dyed-in-the-wool NCO like me. It would be easy to accept there and then, but I am haunted by the memory of a man who shared a secret with me, and now has only half a life. True, I gave no promise, nor assumed any obligation, but he would expect me to do the right thing without that.

'There is one other thing, sir,' I say without looking up.

'What is that?'

'It concerns Mr Welks and Sub-Lieutenant Billings.'

I raise my eyes and watch them look at each other. Tyson speaks in level tones. 'I don't think we need go into that, Grant. Mr Welks is leaving us at Singapore, and we are not likely to see much of him before then. He has devoted himself to working day and night to ensure that there will be no repetition of the various malfunctions that have occurred on the way out from England. In fact he is so determined, he is taking all his meals in the engine-room, and refuses to take advantage of wardroom facilities. Neither the captain or myself see any reason to try and persuade him otherwise, and I do not think anything will be gained by bringing new revelations into the limelight. For him, or for Subby.'

I look down at my glass. The remains of the tot goes down in one gulp and I set it down firmly on the table. 'That's all I have to tell you, sir.'

Studding smiles. 'Do we get an invitation to the wedding then?' he asks with a slight chuckle. 'After all, that is what made you consider promotion in the first place, was it not?'

I lean back to sit bolt upright. The warmth of the pressure hull brings beads of sweat to my brow, and I can hear the breathing of the air-conditioner. Zoe's face takes a vague form in my mind for the first time in a long while. It is a face that can make my inside melt. For a moment I feel a lump of lead weighing deep in my gut. The die is cast. The strings are pulled, and with the commendations put forward by Studding only a miracle can stop me becoming an officer. He, Calvin and Kevel have worked it all out between them.

A sudden flint-sharp image of Zoe's face flashes through my mind. I remember what it is like to hold her, and there is a knot inside that aches like hell.

I wrench the image away. 'No, sir. This new job is all I need. I shall devote all my energies to it.' I smile at him. 'I suppose that deep down I am not the marrying kind.'

His face sets hard. 'You are dismissed, Grant,' he snarls, and his tone brings a look of alarm from Tyson.

Two more Ben Grant novels by Eric J. Collenette

THE MONDAY MUTINY

The war is over. But the Navy is still not at peace; it still has a role to play – tracking down illegal Jewish immigrant ships and trying to prevent their reaching Palestine. It is a role in which the men of the sloop *Condor*, including its coxswain Ben Grant, are mere pawns in a political situation over which they have no control. They are torn between their orders and their consciences when such an illegal ship is boarded.

Ben Grant has more to contend with than keeping the lid on a violent situation. And it takes Leading Sick Bay Attendant Monday, who rides the coxswain's back like a conscience, to bring matters to a head.

GRUESOME TIDE

The time is Dunkirk. And Ben Grant is a seasoned submarine coxswain, experienced but as yet unbloodied in war. That is not to be long in coming. Taking with him fellow submariner Stoker Albert Finney, he volunteers for duty at Dunkirk and takes across a shuitje – a cross between a Thames barge and a small coaster. When he arrives at the beaches he is ordered to abandon her there and join Lieutenant Martingale, now in command of the destroyer *Brigand* after the death in action of his skipper. The job is no sinecure. For Martingale is no more a lover of following orders without good reason than is Grant himself, especially when matters of conscience are at stake.

EYE OF THE EAGLE
Eric J. Collenette

It is spring 1944, and the air is heavy with talk of invasion. No one knows when or where it will fall. They do not know it in England, or in Normandy, and least of all do they know it on HM aircraft carrier *Cyclops*. Out in the Atlantic Leading Seaman Mortimer, his enemy the disrated Malloy, and the pilot Lieutenant-Commander Potter have no idea of the part they are to play, or what is to happen to them as they are swept up in the destiny of a small Norman village, caught between the SS and the local Resistance.

Eric Collenette once again presents a fast-moving and action-packed novel of the Second World War.

TARGET: BATTLESHIP
Barry Coward

The battleship was old, poorly armed and on her way to a refit. But first she had a mission – to see the convoy through to beleaguered Malta safely. In the enemy-dominated Mediterranean of 1941 the odds were stacked against them. Odds in the form of U-boats and Stukas.

There was more than mere ships and aircraft at stake. There were the people involved on both sides. The Captain of the battleship, and the woman he left behind in Alexandria; Ingemar Dormann flying Stukas from the Sicilian base; Katerina, the German nurse. Their emotions, their very lives were bound up in the fate of one small convoy that slowly steamed towards its destiny.

In this fast-moving novel of the war at sea, Barry Coward has written a gripping saga, full of dangers, dramas, tragedies and triumphs.

COASTAL
Barry Coward

It is late 1942 and the watershed of the Second World War. But for Mick Hargan, skipper of a Sunderland in an anti-U-boat squadron, for Leading Wren Jilly Johnson, for Helmut Schafer, Staffelkapitän of a staffel of Ju88s, and for the commander of the U-boat: their armageddon was yet to come. The Battle of the Atlantic was about to enter its most savage and vital stage. It was a drama in which all were to become dramatically involved.

Following the success of *Target: Battleship*, Barry Coward has produced another fast-moving, gripping story from the war. This time it is with Coastal Command and the bitter battles between the U-boats, the Sunderlands and the enemy fighters waging a war in which the stake was Britain's survival.